These
Are
Our
Demands

ALSO BY MATTHEW PITT

Attention Please Now

These Are Our Demands

stories

Matthew Pitt

FERRY STREET BOOKS

FERRY STREET BOOKS

an imprint of Engine Books
PO Box 44167
Indianapolis, IN 46244
enginebooks.org

Also available in hardcover and eBook formats from Engine Books.

10 9 8 7 6 5 4 3 2 1

ISBN: 978-1-938126-37-6

Library of Congress Control Number: TK

For Kimberly, Celia, Nina—and all they bring to light

CONTENTS

WHERE YOU GET AHEAD OF YOURSELF

IN THREE SECONDS, PAUL Prezinski will bite a rotten portion of an otherwise perfect peach. Only he won't, because now Paul knows to tilt it and nibble around the wormy region. In three seconds, a tiny flying insect will dive—drawn to the fruit—at his left ear. Only it never gets there. Alerted to the bug, Paul conquers it with a clapping of hands. In three seconds, Paul will prick his thumb with a thin metal point.

Well, certain futures can't be steered clear of. Much of what Paul sees he can't stop, only gird against. He has his hero moments—moments are all we are talking about here—but is useless with needle and thread. After sticking himself a fourth time, Paul gives up trying to sew his own costume. He squeezes from his thumb a bead of blood. It spills a crimson path down his skin. A volcano for an ant.

Honestly there's little reason for the costume. Paul's unmasked face and name have appeared already on numerous newscasts. Still, he's decided to continue his heroism in a costume, in the hopes it will make Paul appear more legitimate to those cutting his checks. That it will ward off the envy of the public at large. Paul's apartment, as luck has it, lies in the shadow of an ironic shop selling superhero provisions. He polishes off his plump peach and steps inside the emporium, where he encounters a rack of garish capes, cowls, and tights.

Spandex is out, given Paul's lanky thighs, his shoulders that, though broad, slope like a wire hanger. Luckily, the store's inventory suits all body types: The place caters mostly to computer programmers whose lone superpower is to make heaps of money, allowing them to make shrines of their nostalgia, keeping mint condition issues inside plastic sleeves and humidors. These lovers of comic lore argue the merits of this inker, that storyline, and can pinpoint the precise issue when The Justice League jumped the shark.

Paul was never this kind of believer. Sure, as a boy he owned a stack of comics, but they featured heroes from his native land. Of famous U.S. cartoons, he glanced at Spidey and Superman; liked his *Mad*, enjoyed his *Cracked*. Preferred comedy to narrowly prevented catastrophe. The comedy now is that Paul possesses a power of his own, an ability to predict the near future. The ludicrously limited near future. And while this has prevented a catastrophe or two, the power has proven less practical than bewildering. After all, he can see only three seconds beyond the rest of us.

In the store, Paul's head fills with a buzz. Fire. He senses fire. Just as he edges toward the extinguisher, Paul sees an employee igniting a Zippo at the register, and relaxes.

"Mind if I take my smoke break soon, man?" the employee asks his manager.

"Long as it's past 4:00."

Paul rushes to the register holding a suit embellished with purple swirls and lightning bolts. "Is already four? Oh, I look here too long. I am late for lesson."

"No biggie," assures the smoker, ringing Paul up. "You'll just fly there, right?"

Paul grabs his shopping sack and hops on a bus, hoping to not miss a minute of Maddy's lesson. Maddy is Paul's private English tutor. She works in a ragged building in the city's Eastern European district. Most buildings there are gothic, and cast sturdy, imposing shadows on the avenues. Bats are known to skitter from the roofs and belfries. But the tutoring building is simply shabby, a victim of architectural leprosy. Pieces of cheap masonry crumble when Paul presses his hand against the façade.

When Paul enters the fifth-floor office, eight minutes late, Maddy calls out brightly: "You survived your journey."

"Perhaps," Paul responds. "Or but maybe not. This could be hell I am come to."

"Have come to," Maddy corrects, ushering him to her cubicle. This is their joke. The building elevator staggers like an anguished mule. By the time Paul finishes his ride up, his face appears absurdly ashen. Maddy began teasing Paul about it, and they've made it part of the lesson. But she in fact is the source of Paul's face paling twice each week. The first sight of her strips him of oxygen. Maddy is the only presence in the building not shabby, exactly the kind of American he hoped to meet when he plotted his first fantasies of crossing the ocean. Blond. A smile stretched so wide it must hurt her face. Sun-damaged skin. A fast talker who deftly decelerates in Paul's presence.

Almost all of it with her is perfect. But not quite.

"Did you finish your outfit? Ooh, looks like it finished you," she adds, peering at the assortment of Band-Aids carpeting Paul's fingers.

"Yes. I give up and buy instead. Good American shopper."

"Hey, it's all about effort. Me, I'm still working on booties for my friend's baby—who's starting kindergarten next fall. What else is keeping you busy, Paul P.?"

"Not much. This was thrill of my day." Spider-Man, Paul recalls from his comic reading years, was fond of saying, "With great power, comes great responsibility." And with limited power, Paul is learning, comes great boredom. Must be how monarchs feel. And most U.S. vice presidents.

Maddy asks if she can see his purchase. Paul drapes the costume over a frame on his teacher's desk. Inside that frame is a picture of Maddy's lover. Paul relishes covering the framed face's scruffy hair, dimple, and mouse-tail mustache, as though suffocating it with a blanket.

"So does this suit mean you're becoming our government's new secret weapon?" Maddy is aware of Paul's power. But to his relief, she treads the subject lightly. When you see three seconds into the future, people bomb you with three lifetimes' worth of questions. Paul never knows the answers. He didn't when the first government officials contacted him, or when the INS fast-tracked his U.S. citizenship.

"No. I am lost cause. They ran on me very big tests last month. As you know." In his native tongue he confides how they led him into a bare, cavernous space like a museum wing with its collection missing. After he'd settled in they'd sprung a series of snares and threats at him through various doors and air vents, calculating Paul's response time, and ability to preinterpret what had yet to be made visible. He found the formality of their approach fascinating—as if they'd assessed similar cases for decades. During the battery of trials he raised the examiners' hopes on occasion—he could not read English, but he could read their faces. They told Paul later he'd predicted certain dangers a full five seconds before their release: a suitcase bomb, a shove in someone's back, a remote-control plane's nosedive. The testers grew certain Paul's ability was a muscle. One that, with exercise, could become more potent. But eventually the altitude of Paul's precognition sunk back to its normal level. "Their plans," he concludes, chancing English, "were premad. No wait. Premade, premedicated…?"

"Back up. What's the word's meaning?"

"Uh. Where you get ahead of yourself."

"Oh. *Premature*."

"Yes. Their belief in my powers was premature. Their plans premature also. Also their faith in me."

If he could've seen into the future deeply enough then to know he couldn't see it deeply at all, Paul swears that he would have spared everyone the disappointment. Of course, in that case, he wouldn't have disappointed a soul.

In the lesson's second hour, Maddy commends Paul's homework, glancing chronically, and not quite as discreetly as she thinks, at her voice mail's dim in-box light. "The sentences you composed are excellent. Perfect placement of the object in each.

You made one little mistake with a verb. Right here. This isn't future tense. But I had to look hard to find it."

He nods, but is distracted. Look hard? He knows these words but not the idiom. Does she mean when she spotted the error her face hardened with annoyance? This does not seem like her, but he is always anxious not to displease Maddy. Around her he must check his thoughts, gestures, and, certainly, his speech. Maddy has told him to speak freely. That she won't judge his mistakes. She tells Paul she'll translate whatever he is curious about: on TV, the radio, the street. That he could never say a word to offend her.

But he could.

"Speaking of premature plans," Maddy says, scowling at her computer screen. "Eli e-mailed to bail on our plans for tonight. Unreal. He's got to settle up with the investors backing his new business. So now I don't get to see either the Heckel or Anish Kapoor exhibits." Maddy looked up from her monitor, toward Paul. "You'd never go back on your word with me, Paul."

"…Of course no," he stammers.

"You like Heckel's work?"

He opens his lips but no sound escapes, as if some stone in his Adam's apple is blocking the words' escape and expression. "I…do not know of it," he finally manages. "But I do know there are few greater joys than watching a beautiful woman marvel at the beauty of something else."

"Hmm. I'll stay here an extra hour if you lob lines like that. Should we move to vocabulary exercises? Or do you want to tell stories about home?"

Home. If he has that choice, always home.

He dials up romantic details about his two-room schoolhouse, the public fountain he splashed in each August, the loaf-shaped hills beyond his town. What an unforeseeable pleasure it's turned out to be, spending some of the sessions looking back in time. Willfully ignoring what happens next. He mentions how he mastered chess as a child. Predicting opponents' moves, sometimes Paul would think no, he surely won't leave his bishop unprotected.

But the opponent's move always corresponded with the images in Paul's head. Images, he explains, which take the form of old flopping filmstrip. Neat slices of next waving within his brain. The bigger picture, he knows, is not so neat. A few times when his father opened his liquor cabinet to empty bottles, he'd box young Paul with the bottles' glass bodies. "The worst part of these beatings is that I saw each blow before it landed. As if he were bashing my head twice as much. The visions surrounded me, confused me, so I couldn't fight back." He softens when the talk turns to his mother and the little shop she ran in the town market. She made homemade soaps shaped as hearts, lips, and snowflakes, all filled with scents so majestic they stay stored in his brain. To this day, he still thinks the city smells like almonds, or green apples.

When he returns home there's a message on Paul's machine. His accountant anxiously describing paperwork scrapes, hitches in his tax status. Paul barely comprehends—but there's a universally ominous tone to money troubles. In early April these are thorny issues. For instance: What to call Paul on the 1099? CRUSADER? Not likely. How about Security Specialist?

Another thorn: What was fair market value for Paul's service? Occasionally his rate seemed like a bargain, such as the night Paul, hired to protect a famous rock band, commandeered the tour bus just before the driver had an embolism on the highway. How Paul had been rewarded for his quick action! Slipped into a celebratory backstage party, given a role in the band's next video, invited to binge drink with the drummer.

When Paul regaled Maddy with roadie stories, though, it failed to stoke her envy. And Paul was ashamed to share other tales from the trenches. Collecting cash, for example, from a high school that hired him in the wake of an ugly racist threat. Paul's job was to snuff flare-ups. A month passed. No retaliation occurred. The principal was delighted—but also chagrined, to owe Paul compensation for standing in front of shop class and the science wing. A glorified hall monitor. Still, Paul accepted each and every dollar. His ability as a minute oracle was his only defense against poverty, the villain that pervaded all corners of his new home country.

"What would you do," Maddy asks one evening, over flavorless office coffee, an hour beyond the end of the session. "If you didn't have your niche?"

"My notch?"

"Your ability."

Paul eyes Maddy's phone warily. Waiting for her lover in the frame to call and interrupt their intimate tableau. "Overseas I trained as designer. Of industrial objects. But I only make one model of each object. Prototype, yes?"

"You did the innovation. Then they found ways to make it cheaper."

"Yes. And this was gift people respected." In this country, Paul's résumé sent firms soaring; then his leaden tongue sent him crashing in interviews. Desperate, work visa vanishing, Paul disclosed his peculiar skill to an INS agent, who was swayed to accept the veracity of Paul's claim after he predicted the agent's car backfiring. For a time Paul's gift brought him the respect he craved. But lately he saw only disappointed looks on clients' faces when he accepted his fees—saw the looks, in fact, before the faces made them—and he didn't want to let these believers in heroes down, didn't want their exalted and childish view of fictional supermen to be tainted by their view of a real hero, him.

During the next week's first session Paul lugs in a minor mountain of anxiety. A rent increase has been taped to his doorknob one day after he requested leniency from his landlord. He has scrapped his costume after his latest client asked if Paul did children's parties too. "Sorry?" he says in the cubicle, forgetting himself. Maddy is asking

Paul if seeing the future feels like being in two places at once. In his native tongue he tells her to picture standing with a group of friends. A joke is told. Each friend laughs—except one, who didn't hear the end. So the teller repeats it, while everyone else in the room waits. That's what it's like. Waiting for the world to catch up to where Paul has already been.

"Only, it isn't a joke. What you hear and see," Maddy points out in English.

"No." His predictions, he explains, foretell only what is menacing, and occur only when he stands beside the endangered. An amazing power, but one with a maddening lack of range. Three seconds is not much time to dive through time, reemerge, and caution the target. Particularly when you can't speak the target's language. If Paul's premonition contains any nuance, there's no chance he'll be able to form the sentence in time. That's one of the things he's learning here. How to pare his warnings.

After lunch, he feels a premonition in Maddy's office for the first time. Three seconds later, she begins to sway stiffly in her seat, as though aggrieved. Cups her head with her palms, as if it might roll off without their steadying presence. Roaches in Paul's pantry reel and stagger this way, after he's stung them with poison. "Are you ill?" he asks.

Maddy takes a breath to collect herself. "Don't know. Felt a sick punch in my stomach. Coffee's too strong, maybe?" Sips of tepid water help return color to her face, and after a minute she insists they resume. She even makes a joke of what's happened, deciding to spend the rest of Paul's session learning vocabulary words with a medical theme, in case Paul needs to deliver her to a hospital. Ambulance, illness, prescription.

"Vegetation?" He stares quizzically at the picture on Maddy's latest flashcard. This one has tripped him. "V-v-vexing," he offers.

"Vaccination," she says. "You were close."

"I can be closer," he swears, making sure Maddy sees his smile.

In the weeks that follow, Maddy grows more curious about Paul's vision, the details of this heroism he now finds as shoddy as the tutoring building. "When was the first time you felt the gift? Was it always three seconds? Have you ever saved a life?"

He can't prevent his smile from collapsing a little. And then hers does, too. "Sorry. We should review adverbial modifiers. Am I getting on your nerves? Bothering you, I mean?"

"I know expression, getting on nerves," Paul replies. "But I promise it is not an act you could ever inflict."

"Such a gentleman. And such a liar. I saw you shifting in your seat."

"My mother feels it is—ignoble?—to bark complaints like dog," Paul offers.

"You're too good to be true. Do you have a brother I can set up with my sister?"

He sifts through her request. Why does she ask it this way? Why Paul's brother? Why not ask Paul himself to date the sister? Is it possible Paul has stirred something in Maddy, to the point that she is willing only to turn a surrogate of him over to her sibling? The truth was, if anyone but Maddy asked these questions, he *would* find them invasive. But how can Paul find fault with her inquisition when he continues to scowl at her framed darling? Stare heavily at the net pattern on her stockings? With his slight erection jolting as a fish does when a human approaches its bowl too quickly?

Next they discuss Paul's latest gig: A TV network has hired him to attend an award ceremony. As winners give speeches, Paul will warn producers if they need to bleep expletives or political statements, allowing the broadcast to air live—with Paul as a flesh-and-blood tape delay. Maddy's thrill over this mission is crude and uncontrived. She rattles off actors' autographs she'd love to have, makes Paul swear he'll snap a picture or ten. She promises to look for him during sweeping crowd shots. "And I've got a list of actors I'd like refunds from, for enduring their last few movies."

Paul sips coffee. He was told he could bring along a guest or two to the ceremony. He will be stored in the hot control booth, but Maddy might find the atmosphere glamorous. She's told Paul many times he could say anything. What would be the harm in asking if she wanted to accompany him? If she brought up the framed darling on her desk Paul could show his open palms, claim his invitation was innocent, that of course her darling could come as well. Or maybe at that point it would be best to withdraw the offer. Whatever Paul says, he can't say it now. He'll have to script his sentences at home this week. Practice before his shaving mirror. Such a moment is too fragile to fumble in his mouth.

"Okay, enough prying on my part. That's not what I'm paid for."

"Please, no. If you have any question, always ask me."

She offers her unbearably wide grin that reveals only a glint of teeth. "Actually, I do have one more. What's the highest honor you've received since arriving in the States?"

After he revealed his ability to the government, after being issued a Permanent Resident Card to replace his work visa, Paul earned a seat inside all high-risk presidential motorcades. At first he was made to feel like a great warrior for being part of the detail. Could this country have used you, one Secret Service agent told him, back in Dallas. Or with Lincoln or McKinley.

"In the car with the commander-in-chief," she marveled. "Your pride must've been soaring."

"Mainly," he allowed. "I do share heritage with McKinley's killer. But on this I keep quiet." With Paul on detail, no assassination attempts occurred. And this president has received his share. After earning his initial assignment, Paul was asked to reside in the White House. Several times he sensed when assault rifles were about to be emptied beyond the fence on Pennsylvania Avenue. Too late to yell anything but "Down!" or "Crash!" Soon, though, sour advisors began speculating that Paul's presence was in fact encouraging rogues and miscreants to take potshots in a perverted effort to test Paul's power.

"Ridiculous," Maddy counters. "That's envy talking."

Possibly. Envy was another villain he faced. Partly because of his power—though the public understood that the future constantly rubbing behind one's eyes carried a dense burden they'd just as soon avoid—but more because of the privileges Paul's power gave. The privilege of knowing which arguments would ignite into riots. Which darting eyes meant to menace; which didn't. And the privilege to be adopted, without question, by this country. People envied how his gift had greased the wheel for getting a green card, rapid citizenship, and he could feel this in glares from his wary new countrymen, whether they'd been citizens for six generations or six months. *Why do we need you? Why can't we develop a homegrown hero—to rely on an immigrant! Our president protected by a man who bungles English, who gores verb tenses and pronouns like bulls.*

Paul faced an ugly, private dose of envy each time Maddy took a call from the framed darling, or dusted the pine edges holding the darling's face upright. It embarrassed him to envy how Maddy touched a picture frame. But it was simply done in a manner too tender, too thorough, for him to overlook. How she ignored Paul when she wiped the frame's glass clean was also impossible to ignore.

"These words, *envy* and *jealousy*. Why do they end with *y*?"

"Excuse me," Maddy says, pressing her palm to her head, before dashing down the hall. Minutes later, she returns from the bathroom smelling of spearmint, so even if Paul couldn't hear her coughs and spewing, he would know she'd been sick. She gets ill at most of their sessions now. Paul wonders if the framed man on Maddy's desk notices, or takes proper care of her at home.

This uncertainty concerns Paul, though the concern doesn't stop him from pretending to comprehend Maddy's instructions more slowly, to stretch out his lesson. The longer it lasts, the less time Maddy will spend with her lover. Of course, this also increases the chance she'll be sick in the office. But Paul has convinced himself that Maddy's interest in his exploits keeps her mind off the spells, and any ensuing pain.

•

The next week, Maddy's queries pivot from Paul's powers to his parents. He answers her warmly, pleased by this more intimate bend in their conversation. But puzzled, too: She is curious, yes, but also distracted.

Paul is distracted, too. With the other afternoon tutor on vacation, he and Maddy have the entire floor. And at some point, he plans to grimace at the office coffee, and joke that this caffeine will not keep you up, but it may put you down.

He's worked on the line for days. And also the follow-up, "There is a better café on my block you might enjoy to attend tonight. If you wish to drag on your day with me a little longer." Has rehearsed the word *better* aloud forty-one times, positive at last Maddy will not mistake it for *bitter*. It's okay, he has concluded, to steal her away, or at least to see if she doesn't object. Some women are flattered by such thievery.

"Are your parents," she asks, "still married?" Paul coughs stiffly. Maddy pops a piece of gum into her mouth, and shakes her head. "Sorry. That was direct."

"It cannot be helped. The subject of my father is not one to ease into. He left us when I was a boy." Paul closes his eyes to wake the image. In their suddenly empty home, Paul sang "Sto lat" the night his father left, to try and cheer his mother. They sang it the following year, to mark the abandonment's anniversary, and the next after that. But each year Paul sang, its melody slowed and saddened. "Out of our house with now warning. But not all of him, never all of him. There are days the part of my mind that holds his memory seems at last to have shut down. Shut off? Which would be relief. But the next day, he blinks back. Like flickering light."

"It's wrong for a parent to abandon a child," Maddy says quietly. "What about keeping a parent away from his child. Would that be just as cruel?"

"It depends, yes? If is parent fit to be near child?" Paul's mind fills with a buzz of alarm. This is all wrong. They are talking about Paul's life, but it is only half the story. He suddenly grasps that they are talking about another child too. Paul lifts the framed darling off Maddy's desk; when he does, a last ray of light from a window overlooking the avenue bursts against its glass as if Paul has put it to a flame. "Does he know? About the boy you are carrying?"

Maddy's smile draws down. "Do you see that? That I'm having a boy?"

"I—see you. How you run to restroom, and return smelling like mints. As I say, my mother's job raised me to closely notice scent. I see how you barely touch food, or sip coffee. I see how you talk to him now when he calls on telephone. Jaw set. Eyes turn from his picture."

"He doesn't know. I'm searching for the right time to reveal it." She spits her gum into a tissue and rolls it into a ball. The tissue looks like a soft paper flower. "That's not true. I'm fighting over whether to tell him at all."

"Why would you withhold this news?" Paul asks. He covers a fist with the other hand to stress his next remark. "Does he strike you?"

"Sometimes," she says, sinking into her chair, "I think he will. He might. When he's run out of insults when we argue. When I ask where this money to start his store came from. But no, he never has. And we *do* talk about kids. Having them someday. He swears once he gets his shit together he'll make a good father. I made a pros-and-cons list this weekend. Reasons to stay with him," she explains, off Paul's quizzical look. "Reasons to tell him about the baby. Then a list of reasons to hide it, end it." She balls up a page from her pad. Paul suspects she simply wants to hear crumpling. "Silly, right? Maybe I should hire you. If you stood beside me all day, I'd know before he did if he was going to hit me."

"If I stood beside you all day," Paul says, slowly—though not because of any uncertainty over completing his sentence—"his hand would never reach your face."

"I have such a small window to decide," she says. He asks her to explain this idiom.

"I don't have much time to make my next move," she elaborates, speaking now in Paul's native tongue. "I'm keeping the baby, that much I know. But if I'm going to hide it from him, I need to leave him now. Otherwise he'll know it's his. He'll want a claim on this future. And he'd be right, wouldn't he?"

The invitations Paul planned on tendering to Maddy—coffee, the award show—sour in his stomach. He isn't sure she's correct calling the coming days a window. That implies opportunity, something clear that must be seized. What she is proposing will at best bring on a painful split, at worst, a robbery of someone else's future.

Since the first day Maddy set the picture frame down on her desk, Paul's yearned for her to part ways with the man inside of it. But how can he now counsel her to leave, when even she isn't certain what she'd be fleeing?

"Thank you for this," she says, slower this time, pivoting away from Polish. "For listening. We need to stop, though. Need to move on. We're wasting your lesson."

"We are—conversing in English. Yes?"

She manages one more wide smile: thinner than ever, a crescent moon reclining. But it remains absolutely, enticingly, hers. "You may have scrapped your mask, Paul. But you still deserve to enjoy a secret identity." Paul feels thick, uncertain what Maddy could mean, until she presses her legs against his. Then he knows. And feels thick again. As if she'd caught his thoughts inside her fishnet. In the rear-view mirror of his mind's eye he sees her leaning to kiss him. He cannot see how he will respond. Cannot imagine how the framed darling will respond. And before Paul can decide if this is kryptonite coming, if she is saving his world or ruining her own, before he can resolve anything about this slice of next, the future is, she is, utterly upon him.

THESE ARE OUR DEMANDS

[APRIL 9] "OUR HEARTS go out to you for your loss," insist the callers who claim to have caused it. Their voices are garbled, distorted in a scrim of digital static. Mother has bolted upstairs, chair bobbling behind her, and while Father's face is taut as he holds the phone to his ear, he isn't listening—after nine nights running, he knows the cranks' script cold. After a moment the callers begin describing possible drop-offs and reunions, where to park the car, what to wear, and what could break any brokered deal. They give assurance that the hostages remain in good shape. Eldest daughter eating well. The boy and the baby dressed warmly, right down to their toes.

"You sons of bitches," Mother says, wresting the phone after she returns from checking on the children. "They're in their rooms. They're right *here*." Coey? Check: feet tapping her changing table. Brad? Engaged in a cha-cha with Nestlé, the family's skeptical chocolate lab. Justine? Sitting in pitch dark on her sill, prying her window to hear spring rainfall—a move Mother put a halt to without saying why. "Each night when you call, it takes us maybe a minute to find our kids. So why do you keep swearing you have them?"

"Softer, honey," Father soothes. "Don't let the kids hear." Frenzied, Mother flings the receiver, which unreasonably fails to strike any of the solid objects in its path—the egg timer, a sifter, a corn skewer—as if, in that moment, all are phantasms.

•

[April 30] A pile of nightly calls. Father and Mother's entire month has been this: leaping lightly in a dark forest to convince dread you don't mind that it's tailing you.

On April's last afternoon, Father fishes in the ice cooler and hooks a pale ale. He likes an ad where a group of men grab beers this way while barbecuing, and endeavors for the same effect. But his can, when he pulls its tab, sounds exhausted.

It is a chill spring day—the two are adding to the traffic of life in their garden. Mother wears her red corduroy jacket. She has a thermos of hot chocolate. She strokes the rich moist soil. Perhaps they will plant impatiens.

Flowers are nature's emotional fulcrums—it is difficult to face and work with them without your mood tilting an inch or two sunward. And sure enough, the sweat Mother and Father shed in the garden serves to thaw—if not quite melt—anxiety over the would-be captors. With each seed packet torn their kids seem safer. In fact, there they are now, at the bay window, watching the garden grow from within the house, hopefully oblivious.

Around three, Father complains of a droning in his ear.

"Bees," says Mother, pointing at his crown.

"What?"

"A swarm of honeybees surrounded you; I thought you knew. It's your shampoo. All those botanicals. Mint, lavender, freesia, papaya. They want to pollinate your scalp."

"Beautiful day to putter," calls out the postal carrier, strolling over from the front porch. He was about to feed the family mailbox when he spotted Father, waving wildly at his head. "And you two got such a beautiful yard to do it in."

Distributing the day's mail, he points out a catalog Father's asked about. Father tries not to condemn the carrier's hollow-eyed glances, nor notice that the sandals on his feet surely flout USPS regulations. "See you got dahlias and false indigo. Peonies already look beautiful; what's that you're trying beneath the bay window?"

"Impatiens."

"Ah, yeah." The carrier nods deeply. "Good choice. How those children of yours? Still beautiful as ever?"

"You keep saying beautiful," Father challenges, peat dangling off his fingertips. "What do you mean by *beautiful*?" But the carrier is already assessing orchids along the fenceline, stroking individual petals with a goalless, guileless touch.

[June 18] ...is where we pick up next. Threats to abduct the kids have not abated, but Mother and Father strain to contain them inside the house. On this point of not being transparent, the parents are a united front: better the kids not know, so as not to be knotted with worry. And to not have those knots visible throughout the town, reflecting poorly on Mother and Father's brittle proficiency as protectors.

Brad rumbles downstairs for dinner and surveys the spread. "Spaghetti again?"

"Spaghetti never," Mother corrects, jovially pinching Brad's ear with salad tongs. "We ate fettuccini last week and we'll enjoy linguini now."

Justine shrugs. "It's all noodles." Little Coey, cradled in her arms, all of eleven months, squeals at the sight of lit prim candles on the dining room table.

"Thank you, dear Lord," Father says, hands clutched in prayer, "for double-bolt locks. Iron bars installed in windows and Nestlé's I-mean-business teeth." Mother heels him sharply beneath the table. "God grant serenity for the things I cannot change and the courage to assume I can change anything."

"Ahem," Brad announces, after amens. "Everyone, please observe." He locates the longest linguini noodle, tilts his head back slowly, and slurps down the entire strand, except for the very tip, which he pinches just outside his lips. After a pause for drama, Brad yanks its *al dente* body back from the depths of his throat.

"What," asks Mother, "did you just do?"

MATTHEW PITT

"Amazing, right? You got to surrender and open up. That's what sensei said. Can I get another Amen?"

He gets more, and worse: Within seconds, the curtain of martial law thumps down on Brad's act. He is grounded, told not to talk back, sent to his room when he does, deprived of dinner and other rights.

"'Surrender and open up'?" Mother asks Justine. "Who is this sensei?"

"Remember that all-town picnic we went to? Brad watched the sword swallower's performance six times, and now he wants to learn the trade. Guy told him to practice on pasta."

"Well, no more noodles, if that's how he plans to treat them."

Justine's smirk is a snake closing in on quivering prey. "You can't prevent a person from making magic."

An hour later the parents are edgily expecting the call with each grease streak they wipe off the plates. "Tonight I walked home past the plaza," Father says, chuckling without ardor. "There's a statue of a frontiersman who ended a major conflict with the Cinakota tribe without killing a single man. His ingenious solution was to shoot the natives' feet. Hundreds of Hall rifles left hundreds of Indians lame but alive, and ready to sign any treaty." Seeing that statue always gives Father solace that quick minds can temper brutality. But when he strolled by tonight, he caught a man scaling the statue, legs lasciviously wrapped around its metal torso. He yelled at the guy, but the pervert just climbed higher: hands seizing the bronze collarbone, pelvis pumping at the statue's somber face. Father scanned the plaza for stones. The initial five he launched missed, but the sixth clipped a mourning dove nesting on the hat brim. The bird teetered down, and tumbled, dead, to the base.

"You didn't need to have done that," the creep shouted. "I'd almost shooed the damn thing away."

"Is there a moral here?" Mother asks.

By way of answering, Father fetches a photo album. "The callers don't *have* our children. But we feel they do. We feel they've been taken even while staring directly into their sweet innocent faces. The omens have become more fearsome than the act." He removes a photo taken before this year's Easter services. In it Justine stands on tiptoe, showing off the long legs she feels are her most alluring feature. "In May, they described this dress to a 'T.' They saw how Brad's lapel carnation sent him into a sneezing fit. Who would have that kind of zoom lens into our lives? Teachers, preachers, guy who mows our lawn, two-bit magicians, the mail carrier…"

"The carrier takes an interest in our perennials. He's harmless."

"I'm not *saying* it's the carrier. He's a could-be. They're all could-bes. That's the problem. All this conjecture has worn our nerves down to nubs."

"What's your suggestion?" Mother asks, clicking the dishwasher to heavy soak.

"We have thousands in cash on hand. Maturing bonds. Just listen. These people, if you can call them that, know our kids' dietary needs, their traits, tendencies. They could swoop down anytime. So let's head them off at the pass. Next time they call, we'll agree to one of their demands. Pay a good-faith portion of the ransom."

"Negotiate with them? For…what? Not following through?"

"Look at it in a sophisticated light," Father argues. If they were at his office, he'd use projection screens, twinkling graphics; make a presentation that would sell Mother in moments on its merits. "We're agreeing to a kind of insurance. Like with cars. Don't crash, you keep your premiums low. Don't clutter our lives with terror, we'll make it worth your while."

"You want to do this perpetually? Let them extort us?"

"I'm saying a one-time payoff. Throw the virulent bums a buck in exchange for peace and quiet. For peace of mind."

Mother pours soap in the dishwasher cubby. "You're a piece of work."

•

[July 28] Home from summer holiday! The completion of two weeks of terrific weather, two daily slathers of sunscreen, two daily lake swims, and two meals taken in the charming summer cabin, with a third square in town. The minivan door unhitches, and accumulated amusement racked up on the roadways topples out: truck-stop travel games, magnets and minerals, brochures for river tours Brad uttered ephemeral interest in, pewter miniature coffee carafes inscribed *For Rich or Pourer*.

After the kids file inside, Mother and Father isolate themselves in the breezeway. Call friends, pay outstanding bills, and leaf through newspapers. Wind the stopped clock of the modern world once more.

Father flips to B12. "Does our space program interest you?"

"More so since they started finding new planets. And renouncing the old ones."

"This is about trash. Some enterprising telescope in Utah located a piece of debris floating around Mars. At first it baffled the astronomer. Thing moves like a moon, in a perfect orbit, just below Phobos. But now the safe money says it's a garbage scow uprooted from New Zealand in a typhoon ten years back."

Mother's only reaction is to yawn. "Well I find it worth remarking on," Father says. "Our trash has made it closer to Mars than we have."

"Wait. I haven't fed Coey since we took out the trash," Mother remarks. Then she cocks her head. "Why isn't she drilling holes in our head with her screams? Coey? Justine! Is Coey awake?"

It is not Justine who responds, though, but Nestlé the chocolate lab. Mother and Father follow the lab's whines to the top of the staircase, where the dog is tangled in a hive of yellow police tape; some strips threaded through its jaw, others binding its paws. This note is snared inside one of the knots of tape: *If you want to see the children again—hug, scold, bathe, or tuck them in—you will comply with our upcoming instructions.*

•

"Standard questions first," the detective begins at the breezeway, declining at first to enter the house. "You reported three kidnappings? Justine, fourteen, Brad, eight, and the baby…Coey?"

"Brad had trouble saying Chloe. His version stuck." Mother wishes he'd hurry in, so she can close the door on that killdeer crying in the hedges.

"But they *are* missing persons, right? You really *have* received initial calls from the captors? You aren't yanking our chain?"

"Why would you think…?"

"Precedent," he decrees. "About four point five percent of kidnappings are resolved within an hour of the 911 call. Usually a round of hide-and-seek gone awry. The mortified parents forget to notify us that all's well. Or rather, that all never truly was ill." He turns from the alcove, fanning his hand at a cluster of squad cars crookedly parked across the lawn. "These are Officers Atwell, Mizrahi, Hinshaw, Lyric, Kohl, and Winaker. Past them, Detectives Nosovich, Tuttle, and Joseph."

"I'll never remember all those."

"Nor should you. The only crucial ones are Hinshaw and Atwell, and Nosovich. And me—Detective Clinch. None of the others will engage in substantive dialogue, so don't bother letting their names sauté in your memory."

"What about the one overturning our furniture?"

Clinch looks at a stumpy man lifting an armless settee and allows a chuckle. "Swigert? You're one wily turd. When'd you slip in? Swigert is on special assignment. Governor's task force on fraud."

"Whose fraud?" stammers Mother.

"Hopefully, no one's." Clinch pokes into the house and sniffs. "Smells awfully—Protestant in there. You guys Methodist?"

"Uh…Lutheran. Semi-lapsed."

Clinch grunts. "Yeah, that charts. Caught a bad cold this week. Been swigging mouthwash to keep me alert, but I'm blocked up fierce. You got any Listerine I can…?"

"Excuse me," Mother interjects. "Are you still asking standard questions?"

Clinch touches his nose. "Depends on what my honker reports back to me, doesn't it?" Swigert approaches his superior, asking permission to dismantle baseboards on the home's leeward side. Clinch grants such while opening a becoming handheld wireless device. "So then, let's get up to speed. Your current husband is unemployed?"

"No. Where did you hear that? He designs wood-reinforced plastics."

"Try to confirm," Clinch orders Hinshaw. "Anyway. Your current husband is not the natural father? He's fighting a painkiller dependency. He and his stepchildren have what, strictly speaking, we can categorize as an antagonistic relationship?"

"Father is their father, for all three, and a model one, detective. The only husband I've ever had. And he can't pop ibuprofen without feeling queasy."

"Doesn't mean he won't touch hard junk. Where is he, may I ask, this moment?"

"Searching." Officers and Detectives Atwell *et al.* stop susurrating and eye Mother with sudden distaste. "I mean, it drove him crazy waiting for you, so he went searching for the kidnappers on his own."

"In nineteen point one percent of cases," Clinch says, "that is precisely the wrong step to take."

Father steps inside a corner store that recently relinquished yet another shelf of staple items to make more room for booze. Looking at dairy products, he thinks of Justine's nose. How at times it hooks more to the left, other times right. Its cartilage seems to swivel of its own accord, a weathervane of a nose. How will they aptly convey that quirk on the milk carton?

Father was raised in this town. Sowed his oats here, in the days when bedding women on theater catwalks and picking fights in ice-cream parlors was all part of a callow crusade against boredom. He'd been a rough kid, but not like today's punks. Today's punks shot up on porches; agreed to suicide pacts in text messages. Set fires to cars. Left grim graffiti: *Debra H. likes it hard up her ass.* Why can't they scrawl the urges more demurely, as he had at their age: *I know for a fact Debra H. puts out on occasion?* This is not the essential question dogging him, though. No. That would be: How had he not noticed this once-tony area falling to seed?

[August 1] "If victims aren't retrieved within the first seventy-two hours," Clinch warns, "it's curtains for twenty-eight point three percent of them." Mother and Father blanch. Nosovich whispers in Clinch's ear, perhaps a reminder the kids were swiped nearly eighty-seven hours ago. "Right," adds Clinch, prolonging the word so the "t" that's meant to end it fades away instead. "Like I said: a *two* point eight three percent chance they don't make it. So, a small correction. A little less silver lining in the cloud. But on the other hand, you know, lies, damn lies, and statistics…"

[August 7] The authorities only consult with Father, leaving Mother to stew and brew coffee, disgruntled and stirring sugar. Wasn't her husband a pill-popping fraud ten days ago? While he is not that, he is also not one to *rage, rage against the dying of* et cetera. Nor stand on principle, nor claw and punch injustice. The only "ism" the man ever fought is charisma.

But as she eavesdrops through the frosted den door, it begins to hit her: They've enlisted Father precisely for his shiftlessness. All these authorities do, in between ransom calls, is wax and wonk Socratic, commiserate about the abductors' motives, the roots of a criminal mind. "Could be hardened thugs," one will announce. "Gypsies. Each of us can become a suspect of *something* like that, it's the part of potential no one wants to bring up." Another might add, "Way I see it, it's hard knowing just where the Wolf in all of us lies in wait…" She's heard Father's friends pick apart sporting events and wars this way, as if putting forth a theory or agreeing on strategy is the same thing as following through.

Following through is not the authorities' MO. They cling like barnacles on the bellies of crimes. An armed robbery at the Sweet Liberty Bank, for instance, has been "in progress" for over a year. In that time not a single hostage has been set free. One turned fifty this week; another gave birth to twins. The police keep insisting that emerging victorious from the standoff is imperative, but they don't bother to draw up a schematic for doing so.

That night Mother badgers Father before he can cut the light, so he has to sleep belly-down to elude her face. "Today was productive, don't you agree? Officer Lyric on our sofa, naked from the waist up, until everyone agreed he was more skillet-bellied than pot-bellied. Hinshaw helping us videotape a plea to the captors. With the lens cap on."

Father grasps the bedpost, waits for the rest of her heat lightning.

"Don't you dare let the authorities spin fantasies with our kids at stake," she commands. "Don't let them wait so fucking long for the stars to align that by the time they make their move, it's already dawn."

[August 8] As if monitoring these salty gripes, the authorities tote in the next day an excitable portly psychic. "I am Imogene," she announces, using her hands to form soft humps in the air after speaking each syllable. "Learn please to properly spell and say it. For you will want to rename your children after me once I recover them."

"She's that good," Clinch confirms. "Fully ninety percent of her readings…"

"Every word I speak," Imogene cuts in, and here come her air humps again, "is ripped from next week's headlines. I will lock onto the abductors' auras. Be the dowel pins that reunite your family." She wipes dust flurries off the dining room table. "I clean, too, for an additional charge."

Our current moment is such, Father thinks, handing Imogene a corned beef on rye he made for himself, that we expect our charlatans to be experts, while our experts, to make ends meet, must do double-duty in some other field, as charlatans.

Imogene's small, charmless mouth bites the sandwich, but she will not chew, pushing the beef to the back of her cheeks. "Something is wrong."

"It's mayo and lavender pepper," Father pipes up. "I can scrape it off if—"

"Not the sandwich. Wrong in my mind. Digits. Ten of them; a phone number. Call! Call it now!" The number turns out to belong to an intern at the Center for Disease Control, but Imogene asserts that this is a setback of no consequence.

"Imogene just got promoted to Missing Persons," Atwell explains. "We met back at a bingo parlor last winter. She kept winning payoffs. Thought she was flimflamming the place, but she's as legit as this August sun. When people playing board and card games call her up, she intuits, without seeing the pieces, without even understanding the rules, what moves they need to make to win. What bid to make in bridge. *Syzygy is the password. His battleship is at G-3.* Uncanny."

"Something, by the way, I meant to clear up," Imogene says to Atwell. "If I solve crime, I receive all reward, yes? And is not considered taxable income?"

"Oh, Imogene," Mother moans. "Will we ever have them home again?"

"Eh-MOE-jean," the mystic corrects.

Later that day Detective Nosovich drives Mother and Father to the precinct for a lineup. He carts in a duo of men in business attire. Their hair is cropped and curly. One is thin, wears a mandarin-collared shirt; the other has astigmatism, making his eyes slink and sink. Trading jokes with officers, they open duffel bags bearing the Jamaican flag, remove assorted styling products and henna ink. Within minutes the thin one's transformed himself, sporting cornrows and rows of tattoos; the other has slipped into a do-rag with a painted-on dollar sign, and a knife stabbing the belly of the "$".

They proceed to take erumpent, boisterous strides into the room behind the one-way mirror, howling: "Man get you damn hand off me 'fore I call my loyyah cousin on you faggot ass."

"This shit set up! We ain't know nothin' 'bout no kids. All y'all be fuckin' with the wrong faces!" Shoved into position, the men take quarter turns to the right, snarling.

Mother's wrists hook together, as if these antics have hogtied her. Unable to contain herself, she roars, "Them. It was them!"

The men are sent off, and Mother handed a teacup with scalloped sides. "I don't know why I shouted at number two and number five," Mother says, swigging and collecting herself. "It wasn't them. I've never seen them."

Nosovich refills her cup. "Blaming something tangible versus blaming indistinctly is like summering in Spain versus hanging a poster of Spain in your office. Those guys have no priors, but we bring them in for every violent crime, to help victims vent. Once they're officially cleared, we provide each one a hundred dollars and a hot pasta dinner."

"The authorities," Mother reflects that night, puffing up her pillow, "were active today."

Father closes his paper, considering. "Very."

"Not meticulous, or even careful. But better to be sloppy and showy than mannered and measured."

"Makes you feel things are happening." Father smiles when Mother's hand cups his hip and, as it lingers there, the smile widens. This has become their pillow talk. "It was good of them to bring their bromides."

Before they can kiss, the phone clangs out in the dark. At a late hour when only infants and the insane would interrupt the privacy of bedrooms.

"How will we answer them?" Mother asks. "How will we appease the evil?" And her lips are glowing, her voice moist with anticipation.

[August 10] "At first all they asked for was standard heaps of cash," Hinshaw says, explaining the changing nature of the captors' demands. "Safe passage from the country, vehicles with V8 engines, executive pardons. But last week the more eloquent abductor asked for fresh clothes, diapers. New sneakers with strips of neon. The other one mentioned your kids personally requested those, and added, 'We aren't monsters. We want everyone to come out of this safe.' They submitted prescriptions to fill. Not for them, but Brad. Ragweed season's already started hammering away."

"Your children interest the abductors," pronounces Atwell. "It's almost the reverse of Stockholm syndrome. They're even criticizing your parenting skills."

"What? These lunatics break in our house, snatch our kids, then think they…"

"Point is chief," chides Clinch, "we use it to our advantage."

"What advantage?" Mother contends. She knows the odds now. "At this stage in captivity, seventy-four point seven percent of hostages will have already been harmed in some bodily way."

"Statistics. Don't trust 'em."

"*You?* You quote them right and left like goddamn Bible verses."

"Don't trust God, either. Don't mean I'm above flinging prayers his way."

[August 11] Primary night—various volunteers bombard the home with calls, urging Mother and Father to seek out a polling

place, since no exercise defines our freedom more than voting for vetted candidates who have chiseled away all distinctions between themselves like so much grout. The volunteers sermonize in tones of rigid zealotry. Then comes a call at 6:58. "Have you voted for Drape?"

"What? Hey, wait now, that's out of line," Father replies, happy to have someone to snap at. "You know you aren't allowed to prod voters or endorse specific candidates."

"Cast the vote. Or lose the children one by one." Silence; then seven bursting whistles. "The whale's spouted seven clocks. You got two hours to do it, or…"

The line dies.

Justine's hunkered in an unlit alley, inside a cavernous industrial refrigerator with a discarded door. She watches sludgy liquid waddle like overfed rats down the sewer. Her stomach thrashes hungrily. Her hair reeks of sweat. She feels a peculiar sense of power, stiff and sharp within her. She didn't leave home because she hated it—she left because adults kept daring her to shop around for a better deal. Calling her unruly when she poked their bubble-headed opinions. Calling her precious when she articulated dreams. As if her aspirations are a clownish dress. As if she should be content to let her parents pare her freedoms at their discretion. This year she'd asked Father for a birthday trip to a meditation center in order to feel closer to her shared society, and he'd bought her a police-band radio.

This was all before July. In her Before-July life she'd had no use for that radio, but now it's indispensable. Now she monitors the police with it, to keep a safe distance; living on the run as a grown-up by proxy. All it took to start thriving as an adult was to steal the younger kids. Or steal away with them, at least.

She looks up at a stretched shadow trudging towards her. Even after she sees it's only Brad, taking sunken steps, mumbling regrets, she can feel the sheen of dismay cover her heart. "You called home? Told them to vote for your candidate?"

Brad kicks an empty aerosol can encrusted with dirt. "Turnout's light, and the tracking poll has Drape down two. It's going to be a photo finish. Every vote matters."

"Did you identify yourself? Or stay on the line too long?"

"No, no. But I did say the whale had spouted seven clocks."

Justine reaches for Brad's earlobe, pinching it as she's seen her parents do, both out of love and irritation. There's a locally famous billboard of a gray whale on this pier, advertising Sea King tuna, trout, and crab. Its blowhole spouts at the top of each hour. As a foghorn sounds from the wharf, drenching the alley with sad bovine lowing, Justine imagines playing that very note right now on her cool bed, low A on baritone sax. Playing that note instead of cleaning carrot crust from the corners of Coey's lips, or bathing her in gas station sink basins, or disposing of her cheesy wastes. Justine fleetingly misses her Before-July life. She'd planned to be alone, one boring runaway. When Brad packed his suitcase too, Justine snapped their bathroom soap in two. "This is what happens to kids on the street," she'd said, showing him the halves of the bar. His fealty proved stronger than the soap, and a good thing too; they work better as a pack. Besides, the adults wouldn't have searched as frantically for just her.

Adjusting the volume of the police band radio, Justine surveys her map, hunting for city crawlspaces—she'll have to find a new base of operations, but this is no reason to despair. Unless—she looks up the alley. No pay phone. "Wait, Brad. How did you place your call?"

"That last one came from Justine's cell," Clinch says, his excitement exciting Nestlé, who helps the detective corner Mother and Father. "Not the disposable cell that's been used before. Our nerve center got a weak trace—they're near that whale billboard with the blowhole—but that's only a thin slice of this potato. Service provider reports twenty calls in one week to a number matching Justine's boyfriend's house. Fifty other calls to the private lines of her friends. There's no doubt that what's happened is…"

Imogene bounds in, shaking out a bathmat: "The kids kidnapped themselves!"

[August 13] It's been two whole days since the whale mishap, and though Justine had presumed Brad's blunder would put the kibosh on their adventure, the siblings remain free-and-easy fugitives. They flagged this cab without a hitch, the driver telling monotonous stories into his Bluetooth, toting them wherever their whims decree. Guy probably thinks they're meeting their parents at the mall, to watch workers fold homemade fudge.

If you are born for a role, there is no need to play it. Two nights ago, the vision from her dream had said this, a hazy woman with a heavy accent Justine is now inclined to agree with. During her two weeks of command she has exhibited finesse, foresight, and a parental touch. She looted stores but left barter behind: slid worn sneakers into shoeboxes at the Slipper Citadel, left with newer footwear. She's also swapped clothes, and her glossy city map, for a tube of lip-gloss. Each time the store clerks look away, maybe assuming the kids belong to some vaguely neglectful mom squeezing into pants one size small, or having D'Orsay pumps rung up at another register.

Now they're lunching in a pool hall—because Brad saw someone's onion rings and had to have his own. Never mind the sign warning no one under eighteen: They were waved right in, to eat rings and burgers, to watch countless pool balls, snapping with torque, amble and slide into the very pockets their shooters had predicted.

"Done with our demands," Brad announces, waving the list at Justine. "Just attached the last rider."

Confidence, practice: That is what's keeping them a step ahead. Every adult they come across has been eager to help out. So why not keep using them as accomplices? At least until Justine is absolutely certain she has wrung every gain and benefit that going AWOL can yield. This decided, Justine coaxes a flame from her faulty cigarette lighter, and sets Brad's draft afire.

[August 14] Barbecue weather waltzes in from the Gulf Coast, and Nosovich suggests—since the authorities plan to corral the kids tomorrow—taking advantage of the fair conditions and holding a farewell picnic. Clinch confirms that resolution is a ninety-nine point four four percent mortal lock. Even Imogene adds, "Good omens are roaming." At least that's what it sounds like: It's hard to hear through that surgical mask she's wearing while scouring the bathroom with abrasive solvents.

Pigs on spits spin in the backyard that night. Lotus flowers float in bowls of dark rum. Calypso tunes compete with tree frogs. Detectives dance with subdivision spouses. Father fantasizes about his cook's apron, a gift from the officers, transforming into a magic carpet, lifting him to where he can survey the pre-triumph taking place on his dry, browning lawn. "Have a hot link," he says to Mother, hand raking her hip.

Perhaps just one, drizzled with bourbon, on a toasted bun. She has missed these summer sensations. Reading Father's apron— Don't Get Up in My Grill!—she nips the sausage, listening to two officers argue under the treehouse.

"Why kidnapper?"

Atwell taps his knife to his plate. "What?" he asks, glaring at Hinshaw.

"Kidnapper—it don't make sense. Why not kid*grabber*? More accurate. I mean, are these people making kids nap? Taking naps with kids?"

Atwell pierces a strip of meat, poking it at Hinshaw's nose.

"This is an apple-smoked spare rib. I haven't had one since high school. And you want to talk etymology in the middle of my jubilee?"

When Mother sees Swigert emerge for the first time tonight, lit by citronella candle, she knows he's bearing bad news. He is this outfit's hatchet man. Though she expects her heart to lurch, it continues beating steadily. "Kids paid a guy to fax the demands from a copy shop. They split hours ago."

The authorities dash for the fax machine, though their mirth and chewing barely break stride, as if it's natural to celebrate a war that won't be won. After a brusque page asking for immediate cash considerations, the gritty terms commence:

• You must allow Brad and Coey to select one bedroom wall they can color, paint on, wallpaper, drill holes into, or otherwise dismantle, at will. Justine reserves the right to claim such wall for her own.

• You cannot call what we eat on Wednesdays réchauffé. It's yesterday's meatloaf. Frozen casserole from a week before. We'll no longer tolerate these food airs.

• That night in the cellar, Justine was *quite* aware what you two were smoking. She requires a weekly hit (under your supervision).

• To keep us company you will purchase for us one exotic pet of our choosing—alpaca hermit crab prairie dog, etc.

• Ratio of stick to carrot in your parenting methods currently stands at unacceptable level of 5:1 (13:2 on gift-bearing holidays); upon our return that ratio must decrease to a level of 3:1 (9:2 holidays), or you must augment allowance wage $1.15, per week, per child, every year.

• If he targets hotly contested elections where swing votes might matter, Brad can insist we make politically motivated moves each election cycle.

• Curfew. A nice experiment. We admit it has upside as a deterrent. But from now on consider it "suggested."

• If you see the baby having bad dreams, don't watch and

giggle. Wake her. Rub her feet. Flip her over; do something.

• Justine expects ten weekly hours of driving instruction, executed inside the coupe, not the minivan. Lessons will cease only after license *is in hand.*

• Your policy on babysitting is appalling. As you know. Your agreement to our demands presumes we have *carte blanche* to install new methods.

As page after page spills out of the fax machine tray like white tongues, Hinshaw exclaims, "How long's this list? Indemnity clauses, protection of rights, transfer of rights…What the fuck they need sublicensing rights for?"

If terms are not agreed to within seventy-two hours of receipt, contract is null. If terms fail to satisfy us upon our return, we may void contract, in portions or whole, by quorum (voice vote). Thank you for your prompt attention to the matters contained herein. We remain, despite this friction, Your Loving Children.

Clinch folds the pages as if handling the flag at a military funeral. "I won't tell you how to run your family. But I must inform you that if you cow to these demands, I'm required to advise the governor to send in the National Guard."

[August 15] Mother's not sure when the yard party finally fizzled: not long after the demands arrived, she heard giggles coming from the woods, as neighbors egged on officers to play suck and blow. Something about their house being ceded to these amorous antics freed Mother and Father to pursue their own. In the utility closet, the garage, Coey's room: They screwed half the night in half the house, in a saintly way, an adverb implying not just ecstasy but mutual belief that faith will deliver unto you a kingdom. But faith in what, Mother wonders now, sluggish from endorphins and lubricants—that the current state of affairs will end, or will not?

She assesses the toll on her garden: the peonies, pissed on by partygoers, the crushed carnations. Trampled before they could grow, she thinks, soothing the soil with pats. She is racing between flowerbeds, tending each row only briefly before chugging to other damaged areas.

An uneaten buffalo-meat patty floats like a skiff in the birdbath. On her way to the touch-me-nots, Mother tamps sweat on her eyebrows, wondering if the list the kids submitted was a referendum. On their parenting. Only once did she ever lay a harsh hand on a child. It happened this past summer at the cabin, after Mother scolded Brad for swimming in the lake without supervision. To drive her point home, she'd fabricated a tale about a boy who drowned there the year before. She went too far, describing the peeled skin on the boy's feet where fish nipped his body, and gooey algae strips that had to be unplugged from his stagnant nostrils.

As Brad scampered away, Mother heard a discontented hiss of wind through the cattails, where Justine had watched while tanning her legs. "I'd have handled that better," she said, and Mother wheeled around and slapped her. Justine stalked off, leaving Mother to scrutinize her red palm.

She raises her palm now, thinking of a bullwhip, the power starting at the handle, but by the time the whipping motion is finished, all that speed and torque running to the lash. Her hand absently brushes the impatiens—and the mature seedpods, hungry for fresh soil of their own, explode in her face.

"Will there be anything to eat? They cleaned out the cabin when we finished vacation, remember?"

"They emptied the refrigerator. But not the pantry. We can live on dry goods awhile. Make a stop at the grocery in town."

Brad pushes a popping noise through his lips. This was the way he groused. The Before-July Justine would've punched him if he kept up this noise too long. But that won't fly now. The new Justine has to show restraint and stay calm, has to cradle her brother's concerns and doubts, has to... "Christ, Brad! If you're so afraid of what's coming next, I'll turn the taxi around and drop you off at your Before-July home."

Justine has to make a move. The baby's irritable with diaper rash. Weeks of slinking in shadows are yellowing her skin with jaundice. Brad hasn't eaten well since Drape lost the primary—not that Justine's suitcase was a well-stocked pantry anymore. Low on food, light on sleep, heavy on anxiety: They now resemble hostages despite themselves.

So she commissioned this cab to bring them to Plan B, the summer cabin. Her boyfriend called today, swearing to visit if he can cop a ride from his older sister, a kind of reliance that now feels to Justine like a junkyard relic. Each time the taximeter ticks a new mile, the pit in her stomach widens; this ride will cost the lion's share of their remaining $603.56. But the cabin will make an ideal compound to hole up in until she's bent her parents to her will. The beds there are real. The pillows are not soggy boxes. She can use planks in the woodshed to board up the windows, a padlock for the door. There's a fireplace, should the authorities shut off their heat.

Last night the chubby lady from Justine's dreams reappeared in a cloud of Ajax. Urging her to *only stop running once your transgressions no longer feel fresh.* That won't happen anytime soon. On occasion, when Justine was an only child, her parents wanted time alone, for a date, for a movie, fornication, but couldn't afford a sitter. So they'd simply shuttle her to a random child's party— leaving her at skating rinks, a petting zoo, or a carousel, assuming alert parents were somewhere, and would keep at least half-alert eyes on this kid they couldn't quite place. She'll never forgive them for it, but with Brad simpering beside her, kicking suitcases, she appreciates the impulse. Justine wonders how quickly her parents would agree to terms if they received his little toe in a bubble mailer. In the name of embracing freedom, what could she be driven to do?

•

[*August 16*] Wearing black leather vestments and a gold collar, Imogene leads the adults in Sunday service. She possesses much wisdom, once you learn to recognize her particular brand.

"Knowledge is a dangerous thing," she states in her homily. "Though sadly in short supply." She rubs silver polish on a serving tray before resuming. "Because outer space is limitless, somehow we conceded that the vastness beyond us is richer than the hearts our frail bodies enclose. A mistake. The beyond is a mystery that may or may not be rich. But our desires, friends, are surely rich, and surely no mystery. Who are we not to claim them?"

Imogene's stirring words do resonate for Father, but by dinnertime he can't help himself, and when he sees the stove's pilot light, his thoughts grasp for Coey. "You remember her eyes, don't you, dear?"

Mother's fork claws the peas into a neat, manageable pile. "Coey's eyes? Sure. Did you get enough scallops?"

"I miss them. So tender, but wild too, not like you'd expect from an infant."

"Speaking of tender: You cooked the pasta perfectly tonight."

They barely down one bite before the phone rings. "It's them," Father exclaims, and in his excitement to rise, his knees ram into the table bottom, causing casserole dishes to knock like tectonic plates.

But Mother grasps his wrist before he can break toward the phone. "Let's not pick up. Their calls have grown so painful. And dinner is piping."

"Not pick up? I don't follow."

"Look at the spread we've whipped up: buttered scallops before us, angel hair pasta, snap peas. I'm suggesting we pick the peas over the pain."

"Abjure the children?"

"Just give it tonight." Positioning a cooked angel hair over her gaping mouth, she prepares to let the thin strand of starch spiral slowly down her throat. "Open up and surrender."

FREQUENT FLIERS

ME, LETROY, AND ONE other friend went in on buying this baby a year ago. Eighty-six seater, decommissioned when its discount airline went belly up. After three decades of faithful floating and intra-continental soaring, the jet was chained to a semi and towed to a new location to be gutted for parts. But along the way the rigging snapped and the thing tumbled down this gully. Once that happened, we were able to buy it cheap enough. Only a couple other bidders. There's not many want a busted jet with a cockpit you can't see even treetops from.

Thing can't take us anywhere anymore, but it still gets us plenty of places. Imagine the royal coup, presenting for the pleasure of our girls at the time not some slinky dress or night in a casino, but a whole mode of gotdamn transport.

Our current girls like it too. LeTroy and me don't think these girls will last long, but at least they play stewardess. Ones before didn't. We couldn't convince those ones to loosen. They kept thinking police would raid our bird. Well, okay, say they did. Say they impounded it, welded the hull. How were they gonna move the fucker?

We stab stale pretzel bits from seat pockets for snacks. Moisten them with beers, light joints to improve the taste. Why do they call the feeling stoned when all you feel after smoking is altitude, like you're gaining on, and then overshooting, the atmosphere?

We aren't stoned. We are floating and soaring and cruising.

Dorie, LeTroy's new girl, announces she did it once in a plane lavatory; well, one-half times, actually. We commend her—"Mile High Club!"—wondering what's involved in half a time.

"Before the flight, during a mechanical delay," she adds. "Strictly pre-boarding."

LeTroy and me stay quiet, unsure if her remarks are about the flight or the fuck. "Well shit," Barb (my girl) says, peeling her shirt back. "Can't let you outdo me." She strips to undies, pings a thumb against my zipper. "Let's you and me get some front-seat bucking, pilot."

I race to the cockpit, grab my hat, flip the still-working intercom. "Folks, this is your captain. Kindly take your seats. I illuminated that fasten seat-belt sign. In a few minutes, me and my girl will be shaking out some rough old turbulence."

After, the girls don bikinis, and we splash in the creek. Floating downstream on our backs, hugging seat upholstery. Delivered to our vacation destination.

"So where's this plane take you?"

"Anywhere we damn well desire. Iceland, Scotland, Peru, Netherlands…"

"Is that where you dropped off your friend?"

She's talking about Andre. We don't talk about Andre.

Dorie won't stop, though. "The one who's not with you? Didn't you say another guy went in on this? I don't understand why we never bump into him. Or invite him on trips. He paid for the plane, too, right? Rows 1 through, like, 7, are his."

"Dorie, darn," Barb says, paddling over. "I think their deal's terms went bad." So Dorie finally quiets up, soaks her glistening forehead with creek water. Only now that she's dropped it, LeTroy and me can't. We climb out, fetch towels. Eventually the girls follow. You can't let your rides back to town leave you in a ditch.

Andre was our other partner in the plane escapade. He had

a girl, too. But their thing turned crucial. He cleaned up, stopped just clocking at his job—said he'd become a whole new man, but LeTroy and me mumbled *no, just the asshole part.* Watching a guy who used to be like you go all-of-a-sudden serious looks ridiculous. Andre started saying and doing things for real he used to say and do as jokes.

LeTroy and me shot off his balls when we got high together, but he still yapped: about all the real places we could steer and bank our wings if they really worked. Like he was leader of his own damn heavens.

Andre's wedding was the last time we really talked to him. He went to Cabo—really went—on his honeymoon. Came back only long enough to buy maps and shovel out shit from the house we shared. In the year since, he's sent postcards from Bermuda, Guatemala, bunch of places we used to pretend to be…

But I *told* you I didn't want to talk about this guy. Why didn't you stop me?

Layover done, hungry as hell, we hop in for our lunch meal. Only we forgot to open the exits and air out our jet, so the shrink-wrapped sandwiches stink of baked mayo. LeTroy says let's play Air Marshal. We flip a coin, and I win, so he's gotta play Arab perp. Dorie cranks the speakers for in-flight entertainment, one song piping out on repeat: "It Was a Good Day."

In this game, I get the shotgun. LeTroy's armed with a Spork from our to-go bags. We play several episodes while our girls watch with glee. Dorie times us. How long's it take to disable LeTroy when we're six rows apart? Ten? At opposite ends of the cabin?

Then Barb says, "Now you gotta get LeTroy before he cuts Dorie. But wait! Look out! Here I am, clogging the aisle, stupid tourist digging around the overhead."

Even though I already fucked Barb today I still want to impress her. Racing down the aisle, I vault over a row of seats, only to land in a hole—right where we ripped out a seat cushion to float down the creek. My ankle buckles. I feel it puff like its been snakebit. Injury will lay me out for a week. Worse, I can't pull myself out. My other foot plunged into a seat crack, and the cushion has closed around me. More I twist and yank, more I sink. And the whole cabin is laughing.

"Whoa," says Dorie. "You just, like, vanished there, marshal, in our hour of need."

Barb's in hysterics, too. "So much for that cushion being a trusty flotation device. Thing won't even hold you up in dry dock!"

"Looking at my mirror, not a 'jacker in sight." The song's still going on. I must look like…so not a hero.

Finally, I rip my way free and point the shotgun at LeTroy. "Drop the weapon, towelhead. Back off the lady, got it?" Normally I'd slap him; we'd call it over. But this time I wave and shake the shotgun in a hypnotic, tick-tock way, like the snakes known to slither into our luggage bay.

"Come on baby," says Barb, "don't point at his face."

Dorie adds she's out of harm's way now, in one of those voices where you can't control the shiver. *He dropped the Spork. Surrendered.*

But LeTroy is still smiling, even with my barrel kissing his lips. Which tells me he understands the game in a way the girls never will.

"Hear that? You snatched their sympathy, towelhead. Want to go out a martyr?" I say. "'Cause trust me, you're never flying again."

I tap the barrel against his lips; LeTroy's mouth parts from the bitter metal taste. "I'm grounded? For life? Then shoot me right now, sugarass. Become my damn judge."

I put my finger on the trigger as our ladies scream. Why are they screaming? We already said we came by this gun same way we did the plane: only by virtue of its uselessness. I can pinch the trigger all I want; no way will it unload any lead. So relax, gotdamnit. Relax.

LAYOVER

GEORGE HALE WAS BEGINNING to learn how much an hour could weigh. Three a.m., and where was he? Prowling Himerherter Hall, a college dorm he'd lived in over three decades ago. Flashing academic credentials at the security guard. His ID card said it all: He was a fully funded fellow, *maestro emeritus*, a preposterous title (it sounded like the scientific name for one of Sara's bugs) concocted by his alma mater to woo him back. A blue strip bordering his ID granted him access to each inch of campus grounds.

Yet the guard remained tense. Probably profiling George as an aging man seeking safe harbor in a coed dorm full of young flesh, a man whose eyes seemed too sunk and too gimpy to belong to an artist. Finally George was let in, on the pretense of paying a nostalgic visit to the moldy upright piano in the common lounge. He walked past pizza crust, beer bottles, misspelled campus postings, stopping at Room E-2 and glaring at its door. Judy Winters. Oh, Judy. Would you have dismissed George's overtures had you known he'd amount to this? *Maestro emeritus?*

Pride reverberated down his spine, a sound like a quick strum down the bristles of a drugstore comb. George moved from door to door, recalling the women who'd once lived there and shunned him, as though he were in some receiving line of rejection. Lisa Burns; Cindy Cox; Jacquelyn Hyde (who with George was *always* Hyde).

As George serialized his misfortunes, he felt his sinuses clear. Still, his voyeurism *did* shame him. A little. After all, he was on the company dime. He was supposed to be composing the last movement of an orchestral piece. Instead, he was exhuming his past. No—not exhuming—yanking it by the ear as if it were a petulant child. George opened the lounge door. Instantly, the scent of snuffed cigarettes. The walls were still shipyard gray, though the furniture was new—except for that old lounge piano, relegated, as always, to the corner. George sat on its bench, eyeing the nicks on its keys, as if the instrument had bit its nails: *Talk to me, friend. Give my sound some sign of life.* He launched into a few chords (the sustaining pedal *still* didn't work). He used to draw Lisa and Cindy and Neil Kittles—so many hall mates into this room—with idle tinkling. They'd flop on the sofas, eat fontina from the fridge, then bore quickly. To keep the people from leaving, George would shift from the slower melodies he favored to jazzier riffs; Ellington, Meade Lux Lewis. His trick worked *too* well: His chords cast a spell, and his peers in response cast decorum aside, exchanging looks saturated with infatuation, drinking wine and pairing up, as oblivious to the music as its maker. Once his audience's articles of clothing began to descend to the floor, George stopped playing to retreat, lonely, horny, back to his room for a night of György Cziffra, guacamole, and Gould's impossibly slow *Appassionata.* The Sexual Revolution was here, and somehow George had wound up with an administrative position.

Even Sara, brazen as a brushfire, had eventually spurned him.

But that could change: Today, it could. Sara was in New York City for one night; a Saturday night stay; a layover from her latest jaunt around the world. She'd called George at 2 a.m. Saying she wanted to see him. Saying she knew it was ultra late, ultra short notice, but she knew he'd be awake and available.

He gazed at his cold dinner. A wave of steamed spinach like a bad comb over. A pool of glass noodles that looked tranquil, as if sure he would spare their lives. What, he wondered, did she mean by available? "Of course," he said. "When?"

"Well, I'm catching a nonsked at 9:55." Then he heard her

speaking to someone else, probably into another receiver: "Well I prefer Simons. Not for company, but he knows nocturnal habits better." She was a practitioner of phone bigamy. After speaking sweetly to George on one phone, she'd bark directives into another. This second listener was her employer, the director of a foundation whose mission was to locate and name the millions of animal species that remained unfound and anonymous. Sara's specialty was beetles. Between remarks, George heard masking tape unspool, bottles scrape. The sounds, he presumed, of packing.

"Where can we meet?" George asked. Where do you live, Sara countered. By the Mews. "Kitties? You live *by kitties*?!" She honked at her joke, then detonated at the other caller. "No. Unacceptable. That equipment *has* to be there! Say, George. What about the park? I'll be stewing in a jungle starting tomorrow. A wintry send-off appeals to me. Besides, the park would be the perfect place for Mandy to roam."

They'd meet in two hours. That would give George time to shower, shave, select a new shirt, and rehearse for Sara the feverish devotional he intended, finally, to confess. He blew through his to-do list in record time, except for the change of clothes. When he pulled apart his closet doors, all he saw was a mass of earth-toned fabrics. He said, "You are not my friends."

In his own hapless heyday, he'd only wanted a woman for a few reasons. The obvious, and then the not-so: He wanted someone to drag him to occasional parties. Someone to remind him when he was low on underwear and socks. And he wanted a permanent view of beauty, for those rare moments when, thirsting inspiration, he rose from his Steinway. But now his work was always thirsting—the connection with his craft just a ghost who visits only in snatches and boos—and so his quest for muse and mate had intensified. He felt he was crawling a desert; dry, desperate, aware of the fate awaiting him—but what else could he do but beg for sips of water?

•

The first thing George saw, when he embraced Sara, was a blue inkspot halfway down her neck. "Wearing our work?" he teased, ringing a circle around the spot with his finger. She brushed her lips against his finger—an ecstatic transaction that made George's lungs feel large and clean.

"You know," Sara purred, in that sexually off-the-record way of hers, "you could come with. If you're up for a trip. I'm allowed two carry-ons."

George considered if his passport was up to date. Maybe, if he jetted to some exotic destination with her, it would all come spilling out: ink in Sara's pens, George's missing, final musical movement, rapturous feelings. "Speaking of carry-ons...where's your dog? I thought you were bringing Mandy?"

No sooner had he asked than a young woman and an unleashed Belgian Shepherd came into view. George clenched his teeth. At least with the dog he could expect a warm reunion. Sara's daughter, Arianna, was another story. At the sight of George, the dog bounded across frozen puddles—each step exclaiming with a potato chip crunch—and intently licked the same part of George's face Sara had just favored.

"Mandy!" Arianna yelled, closer to George's ears than the canine's. "Get off!"

"Hello, Arianna." To avoid looking at the girl, George nuzzled the dog. "I wasn't told I'd have the honor."

"Me neither."

The two glanced at Sara, but she remained impassive.

"Glad you found it here okay."

"I live two blocks south. But thanks for the concern."

"Right, right, I forget, you're a Village Idiot now. Nothing personal. That's just what your mom and I called the folks here back in our day." George glanced at Arianna sideways. "So you're here," he added. "Living here. But for how long? I read the university plans to buy up your block."

"Rumors fly," Arianna allowed. "But I work too hard to follow them. You know how *that* goes, George."

Arianna taught special needs students at night, photosensitive children, for whom direct contact with light was deadly. She was perfectly suited for the job—she'd never brighten up enough to be a threat.

"According to the article, it's a done deal," said George. "Instead of raising your rent, they'll just be razing."

"George, I couldn't give a shit."

He frowned. *Careful, Arianna. Not so snippy. It's supposed to be peaches and cream between us until your mom turns her back.* Over the years George had stayed in Sara's Ithaca home often; the older Arianna grew, the more strained those stays had grown. During his most recent visit, Arianna, fresh out of grad school, raw and ready to crusade against Earth's cruel parliament (but not, apparently, to pay rent), had shot George private looks suggesting he'd better sleep with one eye open. The next morning, though, she'd been the one to make breakfast. The one to scrape frost from the windshield of George's car.

"We have Arianna to thank for tonight," Sara announced. "She's the one who told me you were in the Village. And told me about your fellowship. She follows your career relentlessly."

"Relentlessly," Arianna agreed, "but not easily. I haven't seen a scrap of press on George in forever. Is that why you came back to campus? Recapture that lost spark?"

"George must go where inspiration strikes," Sara said, smiling. "Art and money, science and love, we all follow the same rule. Location, location, location." Sara liked to summarily dismiss dissension. Hammer her happy moods into the frames of her friends.

"And if he can't get exactly what he wants," added Arianna, "whatever works, works, right?" Arianna, on the other hand, had a taste for blood and a gift for drawing it. The lanyard and knife were never out of her reach. This last stab could be meant for only one target: George's affair with Sara's sister. Yes, Arianna, good, dredge up *that* episode once more. With her, statutes of limitations were endangered species. Like so many of the insects Sara raced against time and nature's eggshell to preserve.

"The school's given me such a generous working climate, I have to force myself to take breaks—since I arrived, I can't compose fast enough."

George's declarations tended to be centaurs of truth and wish. Only the first halves were factual. George has spent all winter straining to locate a solitary burst for an E-flat clarinet section. He wants the notes to sound tortured, but emerge effortlessly. They are to be a bridge, leading to a last document of strings (for a finale he'd already written). An Empyrean sound is what George craves—the highest range of heaven, composed of ineffable light and fire, where God and angels lie in wait for new boarders. To incite this burst, George has tried to manufacture calm. Phone ringer? Off. Food? Get Gristede's to deliver. Press mattresses against the studio's windows and walls. Unplug the humidifier; replace it with an open jar full of water. Have the building super kill his radiator during work hours—night—then switch on his much quieter stove for heat. Wool gloves, holes bitten at the fingertips. With each new scheme came a short-lived edifice of triumph. He'd drink water, followed by fits of vodka, convinced the creative spark would soon ride the rapids of Evian and Absolut down his throat. But no.

"What kind of breaks are you taking?" Arianna laughed, laughter ripe with vinegar. "Long walks along 6th Avenue?"

"Of course."

"Midnight soup at Cozy's?"

"Only for the borscht."

"Obscene bar tabs? Undeclared sophomores?"

"Five minutes." Sara said, her face twisting toward the moon, whose light was being diffused by gray night clouds layered like petticoats. "I gave it five minutes. And you didn't disappoint."

"What?"

"You two, that's what. Your Punch and Judy shit. The sparring and throat shredding I'm supposed to smile through. George demeans Arianna's career path. Arianna muffs the directions to George's premieres and we miss the first movement. I'm tired. Tired of putting up with it." Mandy, sensing the agitation, cocked her head at the angle swimmers use to knock water from their inner ears. "I've come here tonight to say make up. Make nice." She lit a cigarette. "Or I stop talking."

George flicked at a coat button.

Arianna stepped into shadows, concealing any expression from the others.

Sara's Spirit slowly burned.

So, this night wasn't about romance. It was about the three of them. It was about getting caught in a lie. George was sure that his grudge with Arianna had been a secret one. That they'd covered their spiteful hit-and-runs with clean getaways. "Any idea where we should begin?"

"No, George," said Sara. "It's not my filth to clean."

Filth—some choice of word. Sara had said before, many times, that she'd never forgiven George for dating her sister because there was nothing to forgive. It wasn't like George had owed Sara fidelity. She'd smile, then shrug. They were adults. Friends. The sister matter was water under the bridge. So had the water climbed? The bridge crumbled? Had she lied then because she cared then? Could she be made to care again? It all seemed to be the same unaskable question. Buttons of sleet parachuted onto George's eyelashes. So this was how a friendship, and the secret dream for more, would end. In the dead of night, in a custody battle for Sara's affections. "What are you saying? That you won't be saying anything?"

Sara nodded. A gambler's nod. A bluffer's. How had he never seen this?

"All night?" Arianna pressed. "Not a peep? You can't be serious!"

"Look at it this way. My ultimatum came early. You have hours to iron out a truce. On the other hand, you're just blocks from home if you want to escape."

Arianna folded her arms. George struck his hands uselessly

against his pants. No one was doing any escaping just yet. Instead, the three scuffed along the lawn patches of Irving Park. Not sure who was leading, who following. Without comment they passed the park's general blah: chicken wire covering flinty rows of winter hedges, the dog walker's mall on the south side, the central fountain, now closed, just a reservoir of recycled hippies, Frisbees, acoustic guitars, and the man with the plastered grin who calls himself Mr. Chlorine, and claims to be guarding the nuclear key (best as can be told it's the chrome arm of a turntable). Mandy trotted under a lamppost. It looked like a sooty ping-pong ball screwed into a flagpole.

How much does an hour weigh? George peered at his watch. Half past four. He couldn't bear another pound. "Should we, uh, get something to eat?"

"Fine," Arianna said. Yes, of course she'd agree to food. When there was nothing to say and you had to say something, fill the mouth. Let your jaw do the work and stand in for courage and bargaining. "How about *Panini y Pan*?"

"*P&P* doesn't open 'til six," George snapped. "And not many open-all-night places seat animals, house-trained or no. So I'd suggest the hotdog cart."

"Meat?" Arianna blanched. "No chance. I've given it up."

"It's like you come armed with a rifle, Arianna. Taking dead aim at all things fun."

"Fun for some, painful for others."

Sara stroked Mandy's nose, silently, as good as her word to stop uttering them.

"Fine," said Arianna, browbeaten.

George smiled, leading the way to the cart. He felt he and the vendor had forged a unique kinship. Between 4:00 and 4:30 each morning, George came to this cart for a hotdog, dollar bill in hand. And each night, between 4:01 and 4:31, the man got George's order wrong in *exactly* the same way.

Sara paid for a plain dog, then stepped aside. Arianna and

George stared at their choices, such as they were. They looked like a couple shopping for rings to wear to an arranged wedding. Metal rods, curved like floating ribs, speared the wieners. There were two condiment bins. The alabaster glaze of the juice in the first had frozen. Curved white strings of sauerkraut were trapped, like mummified seahorses, in bin number two. A pretzel aquarium, the stand's one vegetarian concession, sat beside the wiener steamer, beneath a heat lamp. All the fat salt pellets had fallen off the pretzel dough, though, making it look like the pretzels were sunbathing on nests of Styrofoam pellets.

Keeping her purchase in a paper sack, Arianna took a tentative nibble.

"So," George was quick to note, "murder over morality after all."

Arianna looked him over with italicized scrutiny. His cologne, his careful part: His motives for tonight had become transparent, and worse, transparent to the wrong set of eyes. "Like that shirt on you, George. You must've had a date today. Or maybe you thought you were going to have one."

His teeth smashed down on the meat. Yet again, the vendor botched his order. *Here's to the consistency of oblivious ears*, thought George, grimacing. As he ate, a Chinese woman walked by the hotdog stand, towing, as she did each night, a shopping cart filled with tin cans. A plastic bag was tied to her hair; extra storage in case she got really lucky. There was a gash on her left thumb, probably from a pull-tab. The skin looked thick and saggy as deadened lips. Seeing her stroll away, George gulped the rest of his Sprite, removed the straw, went over to her, and slowly placed his can at the top of her pile, careful not to disturb the pyramid. Then she was gone again.

The horizon took on a greased, filmy light. Wordless minutes stacked like towers of dirty dishes. George ran with this thought—a busboy scouring plates, not wanting to face the stack, the fact that the plates he was scrubbing now would be back in an hour, just as filthy with the same daily special. Near the fountain, Sara and Mandy played with ice. Sara reached inside her Coke cup, skipped cubes along the pavement, and Mandy chased after them. This wasn't really fetching—the ice melted in Mandy's mouth before her return—it was more like working for your water. When Mandy tired of the game, she turned her face in profile and coiled on her haunches. Then with no order given of any kind, Mandy extended her left paw. Sara placed the last piece of hotdog on top of the paw, and Mandy, with ginger grace, curled it inward, bite balanced the entire journey, until she'd drawn it close enough to pop into her mouth. She chewed—George counted—ten times before swallowing.

"Dog-eat-dog," he marveled. "You've got to take Mandy on TV."

"And she only took basic puppy training," Arianna asserted, off Sara's silence. "With Mom's travel schedule, she's confined to barracks most of the month. When Mom does come home, Mandy doesn't waste a single gesture." They strolled by the bakery, sniffing for fresh scents. "Still closed, Mom. You still hungry?"

Sara shook her head, but Mandy rocked her nose in the direction of the hotdog cart, and that settled that. They headed back to the vendor at a slightly slower pace this time, crossing cobblestone rotaries that enclosed shagbark hickories. George gazed at the stones. They'd been repaved since his student days. They used to be in concentric circles, spiraling from a clover of four at the center. Now they were cut at harsh angles, like a pie divided by a blind man. The group reached the park's southern side. There, hugging the curb, was a jet-black sedan. Its ignition turned on then off, on then off. Inside, a man George's age pointed to spots on the dashboard. The teenaged girl beside him nodded each time he pointed. The father was a bleary hostage who knew crucial info and now must talk. Jitters flashed across the girl's face—a mad unprompted smile, a tap of fingers on the gearshift—as she felt, oh, she knew, that in a matter of minutes her youth would capsize, and she would finally be given control of this wheel.

"My job is strange," Sara was saying into her cell phone. (What country was up at this hour?) "Like being an ER doctor in a hospital no one knows."

George sighed; he'd heard variations of this talk before. About the thrill she got rushing to Jakarta to save a stag habitat. Or leaning on a government to preserve a wetland. She has done good work. She has a way of getting strangers to believe in all her exigencies. Of course on occasion she finds something already lost for good. A beetle clinging to, literally, the last tree it could possibly thrive in. Sara can hear, even as she measures mandibles, clear-cutting machines revving in the distance, on a path to shatter the sanctuary of her discovery into a million thoughtless toothpicks.

"Where exactly is your mom off to, anyway?" George asked. "She started her silent treatment before I could ask."

"Belize, I think. But maybe Belarus?"

"Belize," George confirmed. "I remember her saying something about a jungle."

"Mystery solved." Arianna paid for this round of dogs. "What a team we make. So where are *you* headed next?"

"Boston." The word was waxy in his throat. Taking trips to cities, inside their anonymous howl and aggravation, no longer filled him with the energy it once had.

"The Pops? Your new piece?"

"My new piece," he said, shocked by his words as he spoke them, "won't ever see the light of day." Oh, the tunnels of ourselves exhaustion tricks us into revealing. "They're doing the *Variations*."

Arianna laughed. "Not the *Goodbye Variations!*" George had forgotten how subtle the difference was between hearing someone laugh and knowing you had made them laugh. The latter produced a crack of pride across your lips, a happy jig down the spine. "They *do* know you've made other music?"

They *knew*; they just didn't care. They only wanted to hear that one piece of his history, again and again and again, again. He was a toy in the attic they'd outgrown.

George's first trip to Boston had come in 1990. Slightly different circumstances. Reviews mattered. So did notes—so did melodies—and so much more—then. Just before curtain, Sara had sat George down, rich with doubt and flopsweat, in the green room. For comfort, he presumed, for reassurance. But instead of a pep talk, she had launched into a description of the defense mechanisms of Bombardier beetles. Mad scientists of the ecosystem, which, when threatened, churn chemicals in their guts. These chemicals whip and roil until their fear comes bursting from their rears in a scorching, stinging spray.

George had listened, eyeing the room's toilet with a queasiness bordering on lust. It was that luminous, that unstoppable. But somehow, Sara's bizarre story had calmed him. All was well when he took his seat and the curtain rose. He was never sure why.

While slathering the dogs, the vendor kept his gaze on a pocket TV, hung on a hook meant for spatulas, tuned to soccer matches broadcast from meridians away. He wore earphones beneath a wool cap, pumping his fist in joy or agony as the match's momentum swiveled or the umpire allowed yellow-card infractions to pass without comment. As Sarah was doing now, turning a blind eye to the sniping between her daughter and George, forcing the players on the pitch to police their own behavior.

George was familiar with the vendor's shift. Ten hours, plus the time to return his cart and report his night's take. Add six hours sleep, the commute… How could he stand to be removed from loved ones for so long each day, his only human contact making change and making messes of customers' orders? George grew lonely when subway riders beside him moved to other seats. When neighbors' stereos bled the hog-tied rhythms of music he abhorred; or music more catchy; or popular; or passionate; or substantial; or angrier; or more dark or light, than his.

When it was theoretical, that is to say, when he lived in

Warrensburg, Missouri, George believed with all his untested heart in The Immigrant Story. That, once in America, they would all bloom. And they would have a friend in him. Now that he lived around them, though, competing for the same money and sunlight, he no longer believed dock loaders could rewrite themselves into wily market analysts. No longer believed street vendors whose first language wasn't George's could dangle a word like "imprimatur" in a sentence and make it relevant. Since moving to New York, George had come to shortchange everyone's second chance. So why should he expect his own second chance from these two women?

They munched the dogs in the shadow of an Arc de Triomphe replica. The park was less theirs now. Joggers and jokers with bad jobs were beginning to move through it. Homeless men blew Lucky Strikes into cupped hands, recirculating smoke. The Chinese can-lady circled the area more often, her pyramid rising, rattling more as the breezes picked up. It was, perhaps, five by now, but George didn't want to check, didn't want to confirm how little time there was left to ruin. Instead he listened to other people's chatter, noises he willfully barricaded himself against each night.

"Yesterday he said it wouldn't hurt. He was right. So why's it hurt today?"

"What you think you doing? That belong to you?"

"She promised this time she'd ride it out; wouldn't string me along."

"Please could we stop calling this recreational sex? It sounds like we're paying to make love at a campsite."

"Must be quite a feeling, to always look *like a dancer..."*

George turned from the snatches of speech. He spotted Arianna kicking a child's marble along an ice patch. It dropped into a dent in the ice's surface and died.

"I'm an amateur Puritan," Sara asserted into her cell phone. "I let Warren Harding's or Clinton's peccadilloes consume me instead of having my own."

George continued watching Arianna kick around the marble. The tails of her long coat whipped from side to side. He thought of fan blades. And he knew now, suddenly, what he hated about her. Two things, in fact. The first was that bell-shaped chin of hers. The second was that she'd never taken a pair of scissors to her life. She'd never made a stupid choice. Not the kind of stupid you're still paying for in a park thirty years later. She'd never slept with the human equivalent of a three-car pileup.

Sara cradled the receiver to her ear, giggling. "I told you my big triumph. Didn't I? I found a surprise fifth species of *Solidaga*. My line is, 'I've met the fifth beetle.' You should hear me trot out that line at cocktail parties. It's better than a new haircut."

You should be saying these things to me, George wanted to say. Me, not some person in a different time zone, brushing his teeth for bed. I am here. I am here.

"I *am* dating. What, you jealous?"

Of course, in a few hours, George would still be here, but *she* wouldn't. Again. He'd be the one on the phone on the other side of Earth. Again. Variations of separation.

"No, not seriously. A moth guy; it'll never work. The fact I keep having to give myself permission to stay in the relationship tells me that. Like I said, *amateur Puritan*."

"*Imprimatur*," George said, instantly trying to distance himself from the word.

But it was his first spoken word in half an hour, since the word "variations," so it seemed to Arianna freighted with meaning. She moved off the ice patch, squinting at George, as if he'd asked a question she at first found rhetorical but now that it was exposed, saw was not. "Do you think she'll ever stay in one place, in one state, for good?" There it was, the squint again. That tensed chin.

And then it hit him. Arianna's chin wasn't Sara's. He'd never asked Sara whose it was. My God, *he* knew whose it was, though. He knew the father. He tried to conjure other men with chins like Neil Kittles', but this was a chin only Neil Kittles could have passed on. George felt his chest jolt. He looked at Arianna's hair, its ends like curling eyelashes. Maybe it was the hour, dawn's depressing fingers peeling back the sky. Or maybe there was no etiology, and he only said what he did because each moment was a water drop bearing on his forehead. "I didn't sleep with your aunt to make your mother jealous."

Arianna wheeled around. "You didn't *sleep* with her. George. Goddamnit. You two shacked up. For two years."

George folded corners of foil over his hotdog bun, neat as a hospital sheet. Until the foil got too thick to fold. "Believe me. I was more lonely in those two years than…" Three, he silently corrected. Three. It had been three years he'd lived with Sara's sister. He could've laughed: That he would quibble *this* point, his judge's inadvertent slip of the severity of his crime! "I am sorry. I was sorry yesterday. I was saying sorry before you were even old enough to know what a sorry was."

"Don't waste my time with sorries. You could've *done* it, George." Arianna rubbed her fingernail over the vinyl ridges of Mandy's leash. There was that sound again, the strumming of the drugstore comb. The bristles of pride. "Something to keep us together. Followed Mom. Made it work. Made it right. Made her stay."

"At the time, I thought I *was*…"

"Shh. Just—shh. Just say why you didn't do any of it."

"It isn't what you think." He paused to wipe rain from his jaw. "It isn't you."

"Bullshit. You took up with my aunt the minute Mom had me."

As a timeline this was true—after college. He'd seen Sara beneath her graduation robe, bloated with another man's baby, Neil Kittles' baby as life would have it, and felt speechless. "See the center of the park? Used to be filled with benches. We were sitting on one. All of us. Her, me, little you. Three months post-graduation. Two months post-you. You were sound asleep. I was watching cars scream by, wishing they would stay quiet—5th Avenue still cut through the park then. Sara was about to leave with you for Iowa.

Some assistantship in Ames. Until that moment I was happy that Sara had had someone else's baby. Actually happy—I swear. Because I was sure you were going to do what I couldn't. Force her to settle down. Depend on others. On me, maybe. But it wasn't working out like I thought. She was still taking the job, still planning to leave the second you woke up. I was trying to figure out how I could repress my breath, and all the pigeons flapping in our direction, and all the cabs bulleting by. How could I keep you asleep until your flight took off?"

There was more. He'd asked Sara, over the phone that fall, to marry him. Well, not asked outright, but certainly hinted it. An intimated proposal. He recalled it in phrases. Glints of heat. But Sara had stopped his proposal, mid-intimation. She had to hang up. Arianna had just made a mess. If only that mess—Arianna—had been his. He'd tried to will it so when Sara was pregnant, counting off days on his calendar, creating proof that Sara was further along than she was, that she'd skipped her pill that night with him, that Arianna was their cross to bear. He wanted to own up to something, someone, which wasn't his to own. "No."

"No, what?"

"The answer to your question. Sara won't stay in one place, one state, for good. I stopped thinking she would that day in this park." He wiped cold rain from his mouth. "That's when I settled with your aunt. Once your mother floated away."

"Should I skip this flight?" Sara asked. Arianna and George spun to look at her. She was gazing at the sky. Her phone in its case. Had she heard them, or merely worried about bad weather on its way? "I mean, your job, George, your job makes sense. You create beauty. All I do is pry it out of trees and caves and report the findings. But why even bother doing that? Why bother taking Earth's inventory?" She slid on a pair of gloves, as if the temperature had only now started to drop. Then she shivered and smiled. "Maybe I won't decide right now. Maybe I shouldn't decide until the last possible instant. It's like when I graduated, and everyone wanted to know what was next for me? I had no answer. There was none to give. And I liked that." She clenched her fists; the gloves crackled. "I like having no answer."

George wiped more rain away. In an hour or so he'd be back in his studio. There'd be nothing to do with the morning—a technician was coming at ten to needle his piano hammer's felt, take the edge off the sound. Yes. Nothing to do with the morning but think. Which thoughts will these women sail through once they depart? Will the thoughts fit meticulously like a matchstick sculpture? Or will George's mind disagree with him yet again as to what it will and will not filter? Work, yes, melodies, yes, illusions, no. I will not dissolve the illusions you hold dear. Those you have to see.

George suggested they go sit on the bench by the cart, take some shelter from the wind and sleet. If he went there he knew he'd hear the vendor's TV antennae jab against the cart's chrome, creating the tinkling timbre of keys working a door. It was the last note he could recall composing. It would soothe him to return to it now.

They made it halfway when the wind really started kicking. A chilling northerly blew an empty can of ginger ale off the Chinese woman's shopping cart. The can fell in front of her. Wobbled into the street. As she bent to get it, the jet black sedan turned a slick corner a bit too quickly. The can-lady looked up and the sedan lurched. The can-lady bolted in one direction and the car in the other, smashing into the curb, ramping over the sidewalk, where it didn't stop. A welter of strangers and objects scattered from the spot. Mad barks from Mandy. The father wrested the wheel away—tires twisted, the car skidded over cobblestones. The sedan rumbled toward the fountain stairs, a fall that would have crushed, surely, the skulls of both driver and passenger, if not for the hotdog cart. After barreling into the cart, the sedan slowed and came to a halt. Its engine blew an exhausted hiss. A dented backseat door opened with some effort. One of the riders had crawled that way, and emerged. The daughter. Her arms touched the ground. Is she mewling or spitting blood? Is that a split rib jutting against her organs? Her hands raked the dirt, looking for something that tumbled out the door with her. Near-boiling water had scalded the shocked vendor's face. A sticker for a 24-hour locksmith was stuck to his neck. A woman who'd spotted the whole thing sprinted from her row house with a roll of paper towels.

And there it was, sandwiched between the C sharp of the father's flattened face against the steering wheel horn, and the torqued squirt of a squad car siren that a cop switched on then off every few seconds, enough to clear out pedestrians and traffic, but not so much as to rush the world into waking; there it was, precise, scorching, onerous: the sound George has sought.

ABSOLUTELY, I REMEMBER YOU

THEY FOUND HER PLANTED on the porch glider, shivering yet serene on some stormy November night, tail rings of alternating black and taupe, salmon droplet edging one nostril. Their first instinct was shoo—but when this flea-ridden kitten raggedly mewed, the kids came wending out the door to its call. Caterwauling is contagious; soon both children were swearing to delouse the thing, buy her litter and vittles. So on.

Not so fast. Dad accused both children of inch-deep altruism, citing hidden opportunity costs of pet adoption. *Didn't you want to go to ballet camp?* he posed to his daughter; *and you, bicycles don't just buy themselves.* Mom claimed a kitten would be a pox on her sinuses. An outdoors cat, then, the kids countered, collecting washcloth scraps to prove devotion, swaddling her inside a cardboard manger closed on three sides.

The standoff dragged for days. It'll leave leavings, Mom said. Poop and pee, Dad clarified, before adding how cats brought dead offerings to doorsteps. Bugs, mice, birds. The parents never passed on a chance to make this scrawny creature sound like an insidious hobgoblin, capable of ruining entire living room sets and waking all who slept in a two-mile radius of its howl. Plus, other cats will chase her back here. Why? The kids wanted to know, and Mom, not wanting to get into heat, estrus, and all the rest, simply pointed to her nose. Scent. Boy cats will chase her for her scent. It's perfume to them.

And one of those chases, added Dad, will probably end with her run down on some road.

Tactical error: Now the kids wanted kitty all the more. To rescue her from hypothetical hits-and-runs. Protect her from slinking toms. Whiny desire gave way to dazzling Florence Nightingale routines, as the kids transformed the house into a rococo notion of a hospital, pinning Band-Aids of every shape and stripe to walls, in case of sudden feline emergency, and filling each corner of their bedroom with blankets, gauze, and hot-water bottles.

The parents sighed. Okay: They saw how the feline could be a buffer. How taking her into their home might ameliorate the fact that soon they might not have a stable home to offer. They had been bandying terms of separation. Discussing the whole thing freely, even proudly, in therapy: How exuberant they were, describing their marriage's lack of vigor! Ten days shy of Christmas, they still needed to get the kids a big gift. This cat could do the trick: relatively cheap, no assembly required, holding the kids' attention with brief spells of impishness followed by van Winkle-esque slumbers in sunbeams, like a toy with batteries continually being pulled. Taking on a live asset at this stage of the game would be sticky, but…

…in the end they broke down. The kids were so grateful they ceded naming rights. A not entirely welcome honor, as Mom and Dad worried selecting the pet's name would only brew more rancor between them. But they settled on one—Helsinki—quick. They liked calling for Helsinki, stroking her chin, and conjuring false impressions of a city the two had long wanted to visit together, and now knew they never would.

During divorce proceedings, Dad asked for Helsinki. Given his job's travel load, he saw the custody terms on the wall. Perhaps he imagined the cat as deterrence for his own future loneliness; but more likely, he imagined it as living lodestar for his kids' companionship. As long as Helsinki was here and his, wouldn't the kids want to be here and his, as well?

Soon after the dissolution was final, Dad came back to his new condo from six soggy days spent in Osaka's plum rain season, with an enormous case of jetlag and a small pouch of dried squid. Its flakes mixed in the food bowl, dancing on Friskies, but Helsinki did not come for them. When a few floated up in an air current, Dad saw a window left wide open: stupid, stupid. While there was no break-in, there *had* been, it appeared, a breakout. Helsinki had either gone quiet and into hiding, or had just gone.

Dad rifled the condo and listened for mewing. Looked for gleaming eyes beneath couch crevices or atop linen lumps. Nothing. This space now held nothing more than his purchases; it wasn't one he held any purchase on. Several airport lounges were currently more familiar than his current bedroom. Each "airy" touch filling the condo—half-walls, grated catwalks, door-unadorned walkways— meant to make it feel fluid and modern, instead made him feel aged and fractional. "Good morning, this is Cat Tales," played his lone phone message. "We have your new tag, ready for pickup." Right: Since he didn't share his now-ex's allergies, he had let Helsinki roam the condo, unbanded. Had taken sweet time in replacing the collar with one featuring his new address in the engraving. He should've kenneled Helsinki, or asked his pothead neighbor to keep a bloodshot eye on the lookout. Should've sprung for the microchip.

The next morning Dad cast a wide GPS net, hitting all the humane societies in a twenty-mile radius By the afternoon, with his kids coming over for the weekend in hours, stubborn hope gave way to groggy pragmatism. He returned with to-go gumbo in one arm and a replacement kitten in the other, more or less a mirror of the cat that got away. Dad offered the rest of the powdered squid to this new (male) arrival, who nibbled at, then stared into, his inherited bowl, nibbled then stared, as if he couldn't believe the luck.

The real luck and gambles would come, Dad knew, once this knockoff feline was expected to play his role for company.

After the children arrived, and spent a few minutes exploring all the rooms, raiding the refrigerator and speed-flipping through the TV remote (Dad sprung for way more channels than Mom, and stocked the pantry and shelves with much funner food), they shifted focus to New Helsinki.

"You miss us, cat?" asked one.

Dad assured them they couldn't measure how much.

Tail cocked like a hammer before a nail, New Helsinki sized up the strangers, whose scents he'd made faint acquaintance with only an hour before, via their jackets. The cat seemed more charmed by the kids' shoelaces than the kids themselves. Dad's jaw clenched. The sight sent him back to a moment during divorce negotiations, Mom laying out a litany of misgivings, which in turn had sent him back to college, and Jeff Nilder's urgent request to be transferred from the suite they shared. It had been the same stab— embarrassing revelation in the campus housing office; wife detailing to lawyers why she didn't want him for a roommate anymore. And if his kids got snubbed here, that sharp stab would once again…but then New Helsinki brushed his tail along the crouched daughter's face, and everyone grinned and giggled. It was good to have this cat. They needed it. This condo was foreign, unfilled with friends or even potential friends. The kids had to sleep in cots instead of beds. Had no saddle swings or sandbox, no fig tree to play Simon says beneath—the closest thing being a recycling dumpster that smelled like pickled socks. Helsinki softened the rupture of this new arrangement. They'd owned her as a family, before everything changed. Which meant Dad could never tell the kids—not anytime soon—that Helsinki him/herself had changed.

During after-dinner ice cream, New Helsinki hopped onto the table, hungrily circling the son's dish. "Get down," chided the boy, more than a little freaked by this wild-eyed summit.

Why wouldn't he be? Old Helsinki had been demure about food. Had respected boundaries. What was Dad thinking? Bringing in a male cat instead, having no clue of its temperament, able to see, even at first glance, that its new markings were slightly off, and expecting the swap to go smoothly. A deception like putting up a torn mainsail in bad storms: maybe it comforted you, but the wind would not be fooled.

Both kids let the table hop slide, though, reloading spoons with chocolate cherry.

The wet weekend kept the kids listless, indoors, in pajamas, and wanting nothing more than to play with New Helsinki, who appeared eager to prove how little his behavior shared with his predecessor's. Showing zero interest in the iridescent mouse and fishing pole pet one had flipped for. Happy, on the other hand, to let the kids roll him and rub his belly, whereas Old Hel would've dashed away like a shot. "Must want to get," Dad covered, "every moment he can out of you." His kids didn't catch the gender slip. Didn't remark on the ersatz cat's belated mewing (which came, when it finally did come, in short bursts, not a trill). Or how New Hel drank directly from faucet spigots. Or ignored the litter-box to leave indiscriminate scat on the heating and cooling grates.

The children commented on none of it. Seemed to *notice* none of it.

Why hadn't they noticed? Because their excitement for the reunion had blinded them to specific details? Or because the time gap since their last encounter dulled their perceptions *of* those details?

Dad returned his kids with kisses Sunday night, beat. He wanted to kick off his shoes; only the idea of undoing their laces seemed too great a struggle. This was his couch, and sinking ignominiously into it was warranted. This life episode was going to rerun, he saw, each week: empty nest syndrome come early, come often. The fatigue of steering a bond between your own kids which had harmoniously sailed on its own accord for so long, then dropping them off and heading for bumpy, lonely reentry. And the peculiar tragedy of reheated burritos. The condo was cold: again he'd left the window open, but New Helsinki hadn't fled.

There he was, waiting by his bowl, face tilted casually upward. "You did well this weekend," Dad said, not altogether kindly. "Had them fooled."

Dad tossed his car keys into a wooden bowl Mom won in some raffle, and somehow foisted into his side of the settlement, one of a thousand useless things he'd agreed to take—and this one, twice. The cat rubbed against Dad's pants, tail swishing back and forth like a flexible metronome needle. "You don't wanna play with my car keys? They're resting where you like them, on the..." He caught himself. "No, right. That's the one you replaced." New Helsinki bleated at his dish. "Knock it off," Dad commanded. Commandments given to a cat. How hilarious, to think they'd be heeded. "You had plenty this weekend! Spoiled rotten, and it wasn't even you they loved."

Terrible dreams iced Dad's night, coming in a rush, never fully allowing him to slough consciousness. When dawn finally broke, he was unsure whether he'd endured one long, serial nightmare, or slivers from several braiding more tightly each time he turned in his bed.

In the one that finally fetched him awake, he was attending his kids' graduation. Watching them walk, donned in robes and mortarboards, inside a packed arena, collecting diplomas and singing along to *Pomp and Circumstance*. "I've heard the original," an audience member conspired in Dad's ear. "This version sounds nothing like it." And when the graduates filed out, two kittens trailed them, upright tails flaming at the tips like living acolytes. He spotted his children at the banquet afterward, no longer children, fighting over who had more ice cream, but eating crust-less sandwiches and laughing. He poured himself a cup of punch, courage draining as he approached. "Hello you two. You may not be able to place me, but I'm..." He'd stooped over his drink, in a fedora, unable to summon his own name. "But I..."

"We know who you are," the son said, clasping Dad's hands.

His sister nodded. "Absolutely, I remember you." She removed a photo from her purse. "You're in this picture with us. The one Mom hung in our hall. Here we are."

"Here we are," he'd agreed.

Dad tried to do everything on his Monday morning

treadmill—shower, kitchen, newspaper scan—with gusto, as though seizing back routine was identical to losing yourself in it. Read about aftershocks of the 6.4 in Turkey, but instantly couldn't recall how many were missing and how many presumed dead. Read the science section—a Caltech team calculated the weight of all things on top of Earth, that weren't composed of earth itself—but this couldn't keep him from toying ceaselessly at the dream strands. His kids graduating on the same day, never mind their three-year age gap. The fact the diplomas were trophies, or the idea of grads humming Elgar after their walk. Did *Pomp and Circumstance* even have lyrics? And a fedora—what the hell was he doing in that? He hated hats, barely wore them, even when the weather insisted, for the way they misshaped his hair.

When New Hel leapt in his lap, it was all Dad could do to not swat at or box its ears. Instead, he boxed his own. Here he was, cataloguing a dream's improbabilities to avoid head-on impact with its piercing truth. He thought about how his ex had left him all generically marked "his and hers" stuff. When he'd told her, mildly irritated, to at least keep the "hers", her response—"But I'm not *your* hers anymore"—stunned him. She still *felt* like his hers; he'd vowed not to date anyone, post-divorce, for at least six months. Sure he'd sized up women in bars or at meetings, practicing silent approaches, but as soon as he caught an attractive eye, images of ex cut off his view. Which he kind of liked, honestly: fidelity to a failed relationship continuing to track him down. It wouldn't last forever, though. Soon enough a face would emerge, sharing glances and stories containing surface charm, but that also did the work of tamping out old, vivid memories. She already wanted to tamp down, wanted not to wipe fingers on towels that triggered thoughts of him; wanted to wash her dry hands of him. This distancing would work at his kids' memory, too, bit by bit, until the day he became Dad II, Old Helsinki.

It is jarring to have your fate clarified through the damn face of a cat.

Dad grabbed a jacket, gloves, and umbrella—plum rain season had pursued him back West—and assembled the collapsible kennel. The cat hardly looked concerned by this mini-barnraising. Didn't look like he knew he was about to be deported from habits he'd just grown familiar with. "Wanna go on a trip, New Helsinki? Find a new home?" New Hel mewed: tone off, and octave wrong, but Dad understood he was going to recall its warbling long after the mew Old Hel made faded. "An original life. I think you're owed that much." Scooping his unpawed keys from the wooden bowl, Dad bent down to collect this piece of his past, then lose it all over again.

DELTA TRIPTYCH

A THIEF AT EITHER SIDE

MOVING VAN HADN'T MOVED in an hour. So the people who'd piloted and parked it couldn't have just been lost. Clover Towers knew a crisis by sight and this, by God, was one. She teetered on her rocking chair, its legs rising and falling at the pace of chest compressions. She and her brother-in-law, who went by Uncle, peered through the screen porch. The Mather's old place hadn't been worth a glance in years, but on that late afternoon Clover couldn't stop looking. "Those people," she warned, "will torpedo this block. Sink property values six feet under, you watch." She sipped her fifth glass of iced tea, a strong brew, then scowled at Uncle's belittling smile. As if she had said something fanatical. As if she had any need to be exculpated. "It happened before, Uncle. To a town nine, ten miles east. Six families of their very tribe moved there ten years ago. Now were they crooks or shiftless? That I don't claim. But their mere arrival knocked the town off the map inside a year."

"Which town," Uncle asked, opening sweetener packets with his teeth.

"Place called Paunchetto. Eighteen maybe nineteen miles east."

"Never heard of it."

"This is my point."

As a train's throaty whistle bent the silence, Clover added for emphasis, "Entirely off the map."

Again the train whistle knifed the air: the 4:40, growling along the track, a tanker, likely stowing something hazardous, given how the engineer never once eased on the horn. Clover and Uncle gawked through gaps between cars, failing to spot a single figure in the Mathers's debacle of a yard. Clouds seeding an early spring storm kept the sky uncooperatively dim.

When the train did clear at last, the moving van had vanished too.

Once Clover headed in, the neighbors began unpacking boxes from their auto. Nice auto at that, thought Uncle: new model Jap brand, fresh-off-the-lot shine. Clover, he saw, was right about the new arrivals' race. As they filed in and out, Uncle shook his head with chagrin. He didn't have a hitch with blacks. It was Clover they riled—and Clover who riled him. Now she would prattle insufferable predictions night and day. *Paunchetto* this, *Paunchetto* that, like it was the Alamo of her time.

Clover woke on the Saturday after the move-in, her mind in an abrasive fog. Needing reassuring sights, and tying her coarse hair beneath a kerchief, she summoned Uncle. Who shook off the drop cloth covering her pallid, lemony sedan, to take her for her weekly ride. A sedate circuit from carport to cul-de-sac to lunch counter. Finally to the fish market and then back.

The moment this sedan—old enough to not have a rear-window brake light—backed out, Clover's gangly son, Ant, sprang from his room, adjusting his cap, checking to make certain his kin had driven from view. Unfolding a torn, weedy receipt in his jeans, he made a call to the woman. Told her it was clear to come. It still felt strange, exiting his room's threshold or making a phone call casually. He yanked down the squeaky attic ladder, clipping his narrow head on the ceiling as he climbed up. He favored the point of contact. That would swell. That would bruise.

"I love it. The way the colors roll into each other."

That was the woman, Merrell, making this remark, ten minutes after Ant called, looking over what he had for her in the attic. Until

his call, she'd been corralling sugar grains and her morning's tips at
Hash & Burn, the diner where she worked.

Ant nodded, scraping peanuts from his molars. She lived in
the town north, Tulip, with its hatchery and penitentiary and state
college. He appraised her appraising this artwork, passed down by
his dead father. Studying its canvas with such subdued reverence it
seemed she wasn't merely admiring the strokes, but considering the
moment their colors were first finalized in God's eye and let loose
on the world.

"It's a thrilling storm," she said. "Kind you know will stick to
the sky's bones awhile."

"We get those in late summer," Ant chimed. "Usually only
August." He sipped bourbon, buying time to extend his fabrication.
He'd gone to bed with that very canvas nailed to his wall since
adolescence—except for a stretch of six years, seven months—and
never once had he taken its swirls and slashes for a storm.

Merrell's plump hands glided over the gilded frame. Even a
faded sorority sweatshirt couldn't fully conceal her bulk. She was,
Ant guessed, a Tulip girl who'd gone to college hoping a degree
would keep her out of the hatchery. He and his crew had logged
many weekends prowling pubs for women like her. Girls who had
to do low things if they wanted a high time. *Can't read the Greek on
their chests,* Ant's buddy used to brag, *but them signs always translate
into the same two letters: E-Z.*

A question from Merrell snapped Ant from his memory.
"Sorry?"

"I said, 'What happened to your head, Anthony?'"

"Knocked it against something. And call me Ant. So," he said,
pivoting to elude her eyes, "we got a deal or what?"

"I do like the idea of owning a storm I know won't ever strike."

Again Ant studied the canvas he'd slept beside so many years.
Had he never seen the work for what it was? God knows in these
last six years, seven months, his views had broke down and betrayed
him.

"You know," Merrell mentioned, "you're not as young as I imagined you'd be."

He took this to mean a man smelling of bourbon at 11 a.m. was too old to be living in, and peddling things out of, his mamma's home. "Not as young as *I* imagined I'd be, either." Her stare burrowed into his chest, as though intuiting the dark and hateful tats beneath his tee. "I'm unloading my childhood," Ant stammered.

That seemed to assuage her. She got out her purse and said his offer was a fair one. And did he have any bubble wrap?

Within days the blacks were at it. Messing with the Mathers's property. From her perch Clover downed Maalox, smirking at their feeble efforts to spruce the place—a fresh coat of green paint on that tacky railing? Please. Strapping wheels on a dead fish don't make it roll. For their next trick, the blacks razed Ginny Mathers's gimpy garden, carting in new soil. What, dirt that come with the place not good enough for you?

Once they got settled in, though, their alterations grew serious. New mailbox up, two stumps stricken, entire fence assembled. Clover peered at the progress with dread, sighed at their spurious waves when they spotted her peering. "Where they get the money to put up a new fence?" she complained to Ant and Uncle, still waving.

"Don't you mean where they get the audacity?"

To scorn Uncle, Clover emptied the pitcher's remaining contents in her glass, though she wanted only one more sip. Those Mathers should've left the shoddy home to some no-account relative. By dying suddenly, her neighbors had failed her one final time. Course now they give a black man run of the White House— but the DC mess just made Clover cross. This jabbed her ribs. "Had a roofer by, too. Seems suspicious. Money pouring so rashly out their pockets, you got to wonder was it ever lawfully theirs."

"You right. After all, they both leave the house the same time, in different cars. From a garage with no windows, so the cops can't check their plates. Must be knocking over gas stations. One's muscle, one's lookout. Do it in broad daylight even, without even the shame to wear masks. *Sheee-it*: guy even wears a tie and suit out the door."

Clover rocked harder. Uncle fanned his face, begged some iced tea off Ant, and smiled in his direction. "Sure hot for April."

"You ain't lying."

Uncle leaned toward Ant, but Clover knew his words were meant for her. "Not the heat that gets you, though. It's the humility."

Normally Clover slept late and retired early—the dark never saw her. The next day, though, she rose before dawn. Polishing the eagle adorning her mailbox, fretting at its rusted red flag. She'd have to have Ant buy a new box. Brass, steel, some kind of shine that could be seen all the way over the tracks. Then it would be onto upgrading her beloved garden. Before that, she sent Uncle on a snipe hunt for clotted cream, so he wouldn't seize on the coincidence. Her spade felt strangely cool and moist in her hand, as if morning frost had melted there. Soon after she set to work, *they* emerged too, inspecting their sidewalk cracks, muttering. She wished they'd speak louder so she'd know their next move, or so she could summon Ant to quiet them. To explain that their noise chafed his delicate, ailing mother. But all they did was laugh.

Damn that laughing! She wouldn't stand idly by while spook larcenists outdid her legacy. But she was a frail seventy, with only so much energy and money to expend. Since the live oak got sick there'd been little shade to protect her. The trains blistered by too often. And having traded her driver's license for a medical alert bracelet, there was no means for fleeing the heat and noise other than Ant and Uncle. And they'd soon split for good, too: Ant to some new town, Uncle for the new boat he aimed to buy. Leaving Clover alone. Worse than alone, she thought, peering up the block.

She scrubbed bird drop off a Christ statue anchored by the

walkway, her jaw aching, as if she'd been grinding her teeth. The dropping had hardened on His holy shoulder; seeing this pained her, and pained her more that no one was present to see her pain. Our Savior shouldn't have had to die as He did—forsaken at the cross, beaten, in tattered clothes, with a thief at either side. To die for the sake of others was one thing. But to be unable to keep their company in your dying hours…estranged from those who adored you, grouped instead with common robbers who thought themselves your equal—or even your better—this, to Clover's mind, was the worst humiliation.

Her head felt flimsy when she tried to hoe. Her pale breaths wouldn't support the act. She'd wanted her last years to unwind with cruises on the open seas, grace, and grandchildren. But a couple divorces, couple diagnoses, couple slips, couple frauds, couple feuds—the train of misfortunes that freight a life—carried those targets away. Leaving her weak, dazed, and praying her yard work hadn't pushed her pumping heart over the brink.

Above her panic, though, she heard a cord pulling a motor to life. It was Ant. Taking out the mower to tame the lawn. He must have been watching her effort; he must have switched off whatever televised sport had been playing. For her. His gesture proved he saw eye-to-eye with her ordeals. The thought rectified her mind. Fed it the will to bear up under the heat a little longer.

"Honey," Clover said the next morning, glancing out her cracked front door, "that freshly-mown grass smells like heaven."

Ant dipped a pork chop in a Mason jar of applesauce, wondering at Clover's vision of heaven. It would include a bridge game, he was sure. A table full of friends laughing at those still on Earth who'd fallen out of favor. God joining this party halfway through, a gossipy Almighty Host who revealed that those same exact souls had fallen out of *His* favor too, and had damn better well savor their last years beyond the grasp of his eternal and almighty wrath.

Clover refilled Ant's juice glass with a diaphanous smile. He'd climbed back into *her* favor yesterday, with all that lawn work. For once, he was eager to trim up the joint: Merrell had called to say she wanted to stop by again, maybe buy a companion piece of art for her study. One more jolt of cash would move him one step closer to independent living.

"The late service starts soon," said Clover. "If you bring down your robin's egg blue shirt, I could…"

"Mom, no. Ask Uncle for a ride. I can't be taking you to church today."

She set her cup sharply upon its saucer. "Uncle is indisposed. Going to the boat show to put in a bid. Scratch his maritime itch."

Ant inspected brochures stacked on the banister. Uncle was sinking a fortune in a boat? Not some skimpy aluminum John, but a twelve-ton inboard cruiser. How did he plan to make payments on *that*?

Uncle had been a seat warmer at the slot machines at Stage Dive, and other delta casinos, for some time. And he'd mentioned to his nephew having lit upon some streaks of luck in the six years, seven months Ant had been away. One of those streaks, Ant knew, had to do with Clover's solitude. Not long after Ant's dad keeled, Uncle moved in, providing vague comfort to the widow. But in time Clover began seeking comforts from Uncle that were hardly vague. Ant began to guess how Clover's new tenant might have shifted the terms of his living arrangements over time: first agreeing to pay full rent, to help her through lean times, then offering a smaller share once his landlord's longing for him became clear; finally a token twenty thrown in around holidays for gas and electric.

"Well then that's that," Clover said. "I'd drive myself but our sheriff attends First Avenue Nazarene. He sees me operate a vehicle in my condition, he's liable to cite me." Clover's thumbs nudged her teeth. When Ant refused to take her somewhere, she complained by removing her bridgework.

Ant glanced at the hall clock, which still hadn't been reset forward to reflect daylight savings. Merrell would be here in less than an hour. "Jesus, when's the service start? I'll drop you, then pick you up, deal?"

She put her teeth back in, telling Ant as much as he favored his father, it was a shame their spiritual profiles weren't in synch, too. Ant groused silently at this delusion. On Sundays his pops—a trucker specializing in oversized loads—had tossed coins into tollbooth baskets far more often than collection plates.

"Can I at least depend on you to use the leaf blower while I'm gone."

"Yes, Mom."

"I see loose clippings on the walkway. You might…" Ant nodded furious assent, freeing Clover to shunt her request to a new track. "…water the flowerbed by the weathervane…" Another quick, angry nod. "The edging I suppose can if it must wait until Monday, but when it's already that unsightly I'd as soon…" More nods. Then she made a last appeal—with Clover there was always one loony last appeal, to defend against neighbors' whispers—that, while doing yard work, Ant explain to any passersby that his absence in church was due to either a promising job prospect he had to prepare for, or some unforgiving illness he'd contracted. His choice. "So it seems normal," she elaborated, "that you're not with me."

Clover's efforts to boost her property grew more frantic. For every bauble bought for her yard, the blacks up the block installed sprinkler systems, or whirlpools. That she could match them with only cosmetic return fire left her sulking, exhausted. She'd fall asleep in her rocker by twilight, beneath a blanket, dinner not half-eaten.

Meanwhile, more canvases flew out the attic. Merrell now rang the door wearing tailored outfits. Ant for his part answered wearing pleated pants, though he still wore caps to conceal his hairline. On a July visit, Merrell claimed one of the last remaining pictures: a gutter, with remnants of a bird's nest in the drainpipe's curve. Ant charged fifty dollars more than usual. After all, this canvas was in decent condition. Its defects weren't as dramatic, its scars merely on the surface.

Ant still recalled his pop dragging these paintings home. He'd been paid to transport them from New Orleans to a Santa Fe gallery, but his truck jackknifed en route. An accident, claimed the report. But even as a boy, Ant knew better. Company docked his dad's pay, made him foot whatever fees insurance didn't cover. But he didn't care. He'd overheard talk that this artist was an up-and-comer. High rollers soon would seek his pictures. And now he had some in his possession. His to sell as he chose.

It didn't work that way. No serious buyer touched the pieces, with their chinks, slashes, and disfigurements. Ant and his dad patched the least-damaged canvases. In the light of day the two of them couldn't tell a difference between their blue and the artist's, but when they unveiled the frames, collectors acted like they'd laid a fart.

Ant charged Merrell more for this painting for another reason: He could discern all of the piece's subjects, which made it more successful. That was a tree, those were leaf buds, that was a starling, and that, its broken home. "This bird painting always made me sad as a kid," Ant admitted. "All that work she done gone to waste. I don't know its real title, but I called it Broken Nest."

"Well, the nest's not broken," Merrell argued. "It's just half-built."

As Ant studied it anew, she wiped sweat from her brow. It was all heat and no light here. She shed her summer jacket, apologizing as she covered her mushy arms with its fabric. Then apologized for her late arrival. She'd been ticketed on the drive down.

"This really is high-priced art, then." She looked at Ant with a smile that started out encouragingly, then seemed to think better of itself.

"Anyway." Ant paused to steal a sip of bourbon. I got a couple others I might could show you. Long as you here. Of my dad's.

Ranch and farm paintings."

She smiled skeptically. Ant knew she wouldn't buy them by how she touched their frames—the way a diner lays down a napkin after a meal. But Merrell made no move to leave the attic. Instead, she peered at Ant's CD bins. She picked one disc out, beaming. "Oh, this band was the shit back in school. Remember her 'Hissing Highway' video? Where she sang in scarlet spandex, bent over that Porsche hood? That used to be my parlor trick. I'd sing stretched out on friends' hoods and ragtops, *while* the cars were moving. Never tumbled off once, either, even when they drove me over bumps."

Ant tried to imagine her body as one that had once been able to curl over sleek moving metal. Off his gaze, Merrell slung her jacket back over her shoulders. Said she'd better head back to Tulip. She was enrolled in a summer class; was finally going to get that degree.

"Yeah. I was up around there myself several years. 'Til last January, in fact."

"I love it. Didn't you? They've got tons of diversity. Not like here. I mean, with this block, used to be a black family moved in there'd be a war. I don't have to tell you. Least it's changing a little. Are they nice people? Your new neighbors?"

"We haven't formally met."

"What degree did you get? At Tulip?"

"Degree?" He'd been misunderstood, he saw. "Race, uh, history in America."

"And you haven't met your neighbors? You must prefer numbers to fieldwork."

He shook his head. No, he'd done plenty of fieldwork.

"What was your thesis title?" she wanted to know.

"What I called it? Well, I, let me see…"

Ant's face flushed. He shifted his cap, considered his hairline, hurriedly moved it back. He could only remember the name of one essay he'd written, back in high school biology—*Bugs: Why They Strike and Sting*. Merrell stared at him. Expecting an answer. "The

Hate That Has Sustained You," he said at last.

"Hate? Who's doing the hating? I don't..."The phone rang then, coinciding with the bleat of the 11:35. The train's shaking pounded the attic; its railcars could move, thanks to a damaged stretch of track, only at a walking pace.

After three rings, the machine picked up. "Sweetie, when you get me after lunch, be sure to bring my Discover card. Fourth drawer, behind the hose. We're gonna put us up a pretty new gas lamp. Let those thieves across the tracks try topping that."

"My mom has gone, uh, home-improvement happy."

"I've noticed your lawn getting...louder. Lots of weathervanes and benches."

"Yeah." Ant flexed his cap brim. "Hey, listen. Do you think it's a crime to not tell people they're being judged? Stared at like convicts, even when they're not?"

"Is this something from your Tulip project?"

"No. I mean, sort of. Just—say you knew two people. One had done wrong but no one knew. The other *hadn't* done wrong, but everyone imagined he had. Who do you think has it harder: the one being judged by others, or the one self-judging?"

This time no rusty squeal of train wheels saved Ant from awkward silence. Merrell shrugged. Said maybe the question was one Ant should go back to school to figure out. "No. No more school. Now I'm just living." He sealed bubble wrap smartly around Merrell's purchase and gave it a pat. "And saying so long to old pictures."

Uncle was away more often now, carting his newly purchased cruiser to its pier slip, sprucing its dinette with cookware, preparing for a long *bon voyage* ahead. This left Ant to shuttle Clover to church, and then errands, past the North Star market, shuttered twenty years. Faded signs coating the masonry noted the price of potatoes, collards, bread, fish, a reminder to the town of how little all had once cost.

"Remember Tilda Salston?" asked Clover. Ant shook his head. "Minister said she died last night; ten days short of eighty-one. Never thought the harlot would last that long. But it's funny. When men stopped coming after her she brought home cats. That perked her right up. There's compelling proof cats extend human life." Clover sighed. "Think it's worth keeping around something I hate, if it keeps me living longer?"

"You shouldn't keep what you don't want, Mom. Or what don't want you."

She told Ant to drive her by the cemetery. She needed to show him something there. He tensed his jaw as he turned up the boulevard. She was about to get morbid. Not from spotting any specific kin's headstone jutting from the carpet of grass—but after reflecting, aloud, how Ant's time away had nearly pushed *her* to the grave, too.

But when they arrived, she simply surveyed her plot—"Paid in full so you won't worry"—touching the obsequious bouquets. "These are our people," she said. "Won't be long before we're restored to them in Heaven." She paused to rearrange marigolds on Uncle Bart's headstone. When she finished, the petals looked less wilted, more prepared to face the day's heat. "Until that day of glory, though, I want to know you're freer here. You been punished enough these last seven years." She told Ant she was gifting him her house, pure and simple; one signature on a "Transfer of Deed" and it would belong to him, become his property outright. When Clover had mentioned this gift in previous conversations, Ant had rebuffed her, but she believed that home ownership might take some tarnish off his record when he sought work. Her hand lay serenely across her shoulder, so close that Ant thought to stoop to touch it. Then she made the mistake of speaking. Informing him what she'd prayed for in morning service: "That when I pass, you'll inherit better neighbors that what we have now."

"God, Mom…don't start in about…"

"Or that those neighbors will fall behind on payments. Have to forfeit the place."

"What are you wishing hate on total strangers for…get it. Forget it, Ma. Let's go pick out that gas lamp…"

"Oh damn the light. Only worth getting if you keep it glowing when I go."

All you lost was the hate that has sustained you. That line first visited him in Tulip, late in his six year, seven-month stay. He'd woken damp and startled in his grey room, the words coursing like current through his skin. Ant hadn't grasped the line's meaning, but had grasped onto it, repeating it constantly. He figured it at first for a signal he'd let go of ill will toward his ex. They'd spent their brief union slaving for a substance that swore to loosen their pressures, but only loosened their grip on one another. So Ant handled the divorce details personally. Found a guy downtown who did it for $402, a reasonable price for the surgical removal of matrimony. But he'd misinterpreted the line. No longer bound to his ex, she still irritated the shit out of him; in thought even more than sight. This was not the hate to have fled him.

Ant considered what having a deed could mean: living with her longer than hoped. But scrounging more money, too, with the goal of securing a better place for himself. And in due time Clover would be a resident of the plot she'd chosen for herself here. He told Clover he'd sign the document. Agreed to become a homeowner, and to sign the deed in the presence of a notary right away, jaw aching as he said it. "Oh Sweetie, you won't regret it! And won't regret staying with me. We'll beat the place back into form together."

Next day Ant sprung at dawn, shaping the lawn in a shredded tee. An initial hour of clipping and pruning, then the battle to spark the no-good weed eater. Freshen and splatter stuff with the hose. Then trim scruff around the live oak, before it was on to spraying leaves with the blower from lawn to street.

One leaf he swore he recognized from that spring. First to bud, first to fall off. Emerald green in March, now Oxford grey. At the sight of its nervure Ant shivered, thinking of his own collapsed veins. Now he looked at the lawn, level as a pressed shirt except for surface knickknack accumulating on it: floppy windsocks, eagle weathervanes, naked Roman statuary, birdbaths, Jesus figure, white filigree benches, a green reflective globe, and plastic foxes to scare off migrating birds. A history of Western civilization told in tacky trinket triptych.

Ant pulled a baseball from a pocket and played catch with himself. The actual house depressed him too. Washed out brick. Chattering shutters, creamy curtains. His ball eclipsed the sun, blackening it briefly with each toss. Tossing it higher, a thought tumbled into his head.

All of this was now his.

Ant's ball didn't return. A hand snared it from its return descent. The hand belonged to an old, black man. On his reedy forearm was a tattoo of a rake, or else a fork; too faded to say for sure. The ancient stranger thrust the ball beside Ant's alarmed eyes, index and middle fingers atop its stitches.

"See there? This a two-seamer. Never messed with the four. You go straight, you asking for trouble. You want movement."

"Sorry?"

"Doesn't matter what kind. Just be sure it moves."

"Do we, uh, know each other?"

"Look now, I'm teaching something. This a hook. Pitch sat more men down in ballparks than the ushers. See my follow? How the elbow ends at my other side's hip? Means it'll *snap* off. In '42 we played Kansas City. Sun was lashing my skin. Elbow was grease. Their best hitter come up late, sacks crammed, 90 feet from glory, shoot. All I had left was one hook. But I spun him so bad with it, dude struck out *twice*." He laughed at Ant, gave his ball back. "Ain't lying. Dude came to the plate two innings later, ump sent him right back to his bench, said, 'Fool, sit your ass *down*.'"

"Jesus, Dad, what are you doing wandering? You can't be trespassing there."

Ant recognized the man puffing and hustling over the tracks. Though he'd never seen his new neighbor up close, there was no mistaking the line from father to son, even if the son was doughier, his face round as a fishbowl. "It's fine," said Ant. "He hasn't bothered me none."

"You're kind to say so. I'm Bradley Duvall. Flesh of this one's flesh."

"He was talking about curves."

"Course he was. One-track mind at work. Poppa used to pitch."

"Professionally?"

The old man looked indignant. "Gotdamn right, professionally. For the Negro Leagues."

"Please, Poppa! Yeah, Negro Leagues. Bender Duvall holds team records for complete games and fielding percentage."

"And ejections."

"That's the line on your resume I like to leave out."

A leaf floated into Bender's hair. He either didn't feel it land, or didn't care. He had already drifted over and sat on one of the porch rocking chairs, at Ant's invitation.

"Those games were a long time ago," Bradley said. "His mind's hurting. So we came back this year to be with him. But he's not the him I grew up with. Used to be he couldn't go a minute without griping. At us, at how brothers who got called to the show weren't half as good. Now he never brings a bad word to anyone. It's like his bitterness got locked in some closet and his mind plain forgot which."

"I played yard ball for six years. Before moving back here."

"Yeah? Organized or amateur?"

"We were...plenty organized."

"What's the league? Maybe he's heard of it."

"Prison." Ant felt sick saying it, but relieved too. As if the word were a sparrow he had shielded from predators and only now felt safe letting go of.

"Did you, ah, you were a guard there?"

"A robber. Thief. Attempted, anyway. I broke into a house. High. With a buddy. He held a 2x4. I held box-cutters." Ant mopped his mouth—hot as pie from the oven. "House belonged to a black couple. Both of them older than your pops. Both inside."

Bender didn't flinch at Ant's admission. At first Ant figured this was due to shock. Then he saw Bender's attention was focused on a white fence—waiting perhaps for an invisible catcher to flare his fingers, call for the next pitch.

"Soon's we bashed off the outer lock," Ant continued, "the couple sunk to the carpet. Like we'd already struck them. I still hear the lady's shriek when I sliced up their screen door. And I almost did go at her next, almost . . ."

"But," Bradley said, finishing for Ant, "you didn't."

Ant sprinkled Bengal over a live hill, and stirred it with a stick. "No. I didn't. Got me twenty years. Got out in six and change."

"Still steal?" Haven't yet. "Still want to?" No. "Still in touch with this buddy?" Ant shook his head. A cop at the scene snuck behind Ant, drubbing him with a club. Ant heard a gunshot, then nothing else, then came to cuffed in a squad car. Saw his accomplice strapped in a stretcher. But his blood had sprayed everywhere: ounces of it on the porch rail, the drainpipe, the welcome mat. He couldn't be saved.

"Do yourself a favor," said Bradley. "Declare yourself rehabilitated."

Neither man knowing where next to drive the dialogue, Bradley complimented the yard. Ant nodded brusquely. The constant asserting of order that went on here—weed whacking and mowing, pruning and hedging, edging, leaf blowing—was no different from his tasks on work-release chain gangs. Where he'd wear jerseys blazed with fiery orange and pale green stripes, looking like a sickly candy cane.

There, he hadn't minded the work. It kept his head down.

Kept him outdoors, kept him from noting passing vehicles passing judgment. His fellow inmates, black nearly to a man, taught him from the start to not flinch at insults, sprays of beer and spit. To stand tall to the withering gazes and hurled litter. To just keep cleaning.

"Your dad," Ant said to Bradley, taking the hose to wash traces of poison off his hands. "He stays with you, now?"

"That was the plan. But it's too cramped for the three of us. It's made him mean again. That old-folks home though, buffoons and crooks run it. I won't bring him back to that."

"What if he had a place of his own?"

"What if I could blink and drop fifty pounds? No, it's a cross we have to hump. We need him close. But look around. Houses here are collapsing faster than the tenants." He motioned at the yard tools below, the kempt porch. "Yours is about the only one worth saving. But it's obviously already occupied."

Getting Merrell to return hadn't been easy, since she'd already picked clean the pictures she'd been after. In the end he coaxed her by saying another piece had turned up. "Materialized since my last visit?" she'd asked on the phone.

"Shit keeps popping up on our lawn. Applies to attic art too, it appears."

He hustled Merrell up the foldout ladder the next day, and brought out one of his dad's western scenes. The ones his father had actually come to own fair and square. Ant always thought the subject of this one was a band of remarkable cowboys rounding up paints and palominos. But last night he'd laid new eyes on it, eyes that had lived through six years, seven months in Tulip County Penitentiary, cell A2-49L. Now those eyes registered the anxiety in those massive creatures, how viciously the reins around their faces were gripped, and knew: those men were nothing but common horse thieves.

"I'm sorry," Merrell said. "I should've told you before. It's sweet you kept your dad's art around, but his paintings aren't my speed."

"They're mine." Wrapping the work in cellophane, Ant told Merrell he'd signed a lease yesterday. He planned to install this art in his new Tulip apartment. Maybe she could offer advice—over brunch?—about the best places to hang them.

Her face twitched. "Are you asking me out?"

He tried studying her face with no expectations or ember. Knowing she also knew a thing about unwanted gazes. Like that time, Ant guessed, she got ticketed on her drive over to Ant's house. In her youth, her chin dimple and tight outfits probably made officers who pulled her over forget what rate they'd clocked her driving. But that day, she got punished as a plain, and plain-looking, lawbreaker.

"I'm asking," he said, lifting his cap above his brow, "for a fresh pair of eyes."

Ant convinced Clover and Uncle to sit on the porch past dusk, to watch a shower of August meteors plunge into the ocean. But Clover was snoring by seven. Ant covered her with a musty quilt, and began studying Uncle's boat photos. "She's beautiful. Great guest cabin in the midship. Got a name for her?"

"Mast O'Don. First owner was a Donald. Pathetic, right? Ain't even a sailboat."

"So name it what you like."

"I been advised that rechristening would only sic the sea fates on me."

"You shoving out next week?" Uncle nodded. Ant went on. "Shame for you to break this in by yourself, don't you think?"

"What are you on about, Ant?"

Ant cupped the photos like a poker hand. "Listen. I got half a clue how you lived here rent-free while I was jailed. I won't demand the whole story. Main thing is the boat's paid, right? If this house sells while you're away, you still got a bed on the sea?"

"Selling? Clover got a buyer in mind?"

"She doesn't. But I do." In a spree of whispers, Ant told Uncle about signing a lease in Tulip with money made on art sales. About meeting the neighbors at last; about the Negro Leaguer. And how this house—ramps and raised toilets already installed—would be perfect for a shut-in.

"What about the shut-in who already owns this house?"

Ant explained how this house, once the county sent back the papers in a couple weeks, would be his to do with as he pleased. Uncle scoffed. "Clover will sabotage your plan before it gets any wheels. She'd never open the door for an interested black buyer, let alone sell to them."

"That's where you come in. I need to start my life. That old man deserves to close his out in peace. So until Mr. and Mrs. Duvall—that's their names, the Duvalls—close the sale, Mom needs to be away. I figure out to sea is plenty away."

A gust rattling the screen door briefly stirred Clover. But so long as her rocker teetered, her slumber wouldn't break. Uncle batted his baggy earlobe. "You want me to spend my maiden voyage in the open waters, on my new inboard cruiser—my new home, mind you—carting around that woman as cargo? Tell me why in God's name I'd say yes?"

"Funny thing, going over them property papers with the lawyer. I found a rent contract you signed in the stash. It was meant to renew automatically until you moved out. Except the last payment we got on file for you, for any amount, was four years this July. That's a lot of back pay owed. Still. You got a big old boat loan now. So it's debt I just might could forgive, if you do me this favor."

Stirring tea, Uncle pointed at the coiled body, adding twisted snores to their dialogue. Just where would Clover finish *her* life? "With me, in my new apartment. I'll make ten percent over market in the sale, and dote on her with the profit." Uncle snickered, predicting a hell on earth for Ant. Clover would never forgive him for this. Worse, that stubborn mare would nag Ant into his grave.

"I'll deal with Clover fallout," said Ant. "But those few weeks will be the last you'd have to live with her. And the last time you'd have to *see* her was when you docked, and got a front-row look at her face when she saw who'd moved into her cherished white house while you two were out to sea."

In looking at Ant's eyes, Uncle may have discerned a truth or two: how his nephew served six-plus years for a botched crime his botched youth talked him into. How he'd been locked up far longer. Crammed, every day since his plea, beside guys he'd grown up believing to be of a lower grade. Guys he wound up doing chain gang with. Bumming cigs from. Being watched over in the gym by, when he tried to clear more weight than he could press. If that's what Uncle took from this gaze, he didn't let on. He just smiled, shattered a chip of ice, and said, "You do paint a lovely picture."

With that line, Uncle's chest filled like a mast, filled with so much air it seemed he'd float away. But he composed himself; then, and after, when he invited Clover to join him for four weeks in his new boat, rechristened *Paunchetto*, as a way to pay back all her past kindness. Granting her the glory of cracking a champagne bottle against its hull, sweet juice spilling down the sea's very throat. Letting her mutter on the prow as his craft rolled over currents, rocking to waves in dusk's last hour of light. All to arrange for the day she'd first see that Jap auto taking space in her driveway. Uncle even stayed in touch with Ant during the entire journey to sea, so as to time the return for the Duvall's housewarming party.

A DAMN SIGHT

PHONE WENT OFF AROUND three, maybe four; an hour, anyway, only here for sleep and fever. Its peal pinched my airflow. And my brain—logical but Southern—asked in reply to its ring: *What* is *that sound, starting gun for the rapture?* Of course I was a boy when I ceased believing in any rapture but rapture of the deep, a muddle that accosts me during my scuba dives, which this moment felt cousin to. Second ring brought my third thought: *Maybe it's Allie; Allie may not be as chafed at you as you thought.* Followed by, *Last night you said before passing out that Allie was a prison in flesh, now you hope it's her?* My mind had flashed to its ninth notion by the phone's fifth ring, the way thunderclaps lag behind the light that invents them.

I straightened my undershirt, my hello aiming for irritation.

"Asa," the caller replied, in an epicene rasp I couldn't quite place. Or had taken pains to *displace*. "Asa. Asa. Asa." A sound like babble patients repeat for doctors assessing lung quality. But I knew whom the caller meant.

"This isn't he. This is Perry."

"Yas I know *'This isn't he'*. You can answer me. Asa can't no more. He gone."

To this news, I had no reply. Just silent, naked regret. Sweet sweat vapors rose off my blue sheets.

In his heyday, Asa wrote some of Mississippi's milkiest blues tunes. Though these songs spoiled more than spilled. Gone unheard by so many. If he'd ever once set foot in a recording studio, his sound would be living on in homes across the nation. His name, graduated into one of those you know you should know.

Before I could lug up enough words to build a crisp question, the line died.

Three days later I took a plane to a plane to another plane, winging me from DC to Memphis to Jackson to, finally, Baldesta, Miss.: delta town of tin shacks, flaccid roofs. Asa's boyhood town, and mine. Asa's final resting place, and nearly mine. I disembarked from an MD-88 into refrains of heat, forgetting this was a commuter airport with no baggage claim. Nearly walked off without my soft-shell suitcase until a tarmac worker thumped my arm. *Was this mine?* He wore a hunter's orange earmuffs; if they could block propeller grunts, no way would my reply break through. I nodded and left. In a hurry to make my tour as in and out as possible.

Ever since the current budget passed both houses, Baldesta has been Congress's concern. My Corps of Engineers division targeted the town as a "Green Phoenix" site, a municipality of moribund means, dwindling populace, decades past its best, but still shy of ghost-town status. Less a dwelling than a relation hooked to a ventilator. We'd advised shuttering handfuls of such flailing towns. Baldesta was set to enter Phase II. Field agents were to inspect the town soon. If its heartbeat was as faint as surmised, its land deemed by surveyors to be sound, all inhabitants would be relocated. Existing homes and retail dismantled, then transformed into a hydroelectric plant.

Best thing, I claimed to colleagues, that could happen to Baldesta.

A team of grunts three rungs beneath my pay grade was supposed to be here. But after my late-night Asa call, I'd arranged to make the tour myself, mentioning my personal ties to the zip code, and how they'd enable me to efficiently judge whether it was time to wipe the town off the map. This tripped some departmental quibble. All of which passed, once my team saw pictures of the unsightly hole I'd spared them from inspecting. By early afternoon I'd hit Baldesta's main drag, shedding a skin of hot sweat. Strolling in ill-chosen footwear, shoes hard as skulls. Each time I planted down, the ground beneath me squished like sediment in a jug.

Little grocery said it was open. So did our barber. And the catfish counter. But at 2:00 p.m. on a Tuesday, nothing was. A bug of neon coursed through a broadcast tower sign claiming WOEB as *The Voice of Baldesta, Shiver by the River*. But the only motion or sound in the streets was windblown dust. On this anecdotal evidence alone, I could've signed my hometown's death warrant. Nine hundred sixty-one: This is what the latest census made of Baldesta. My division calculated a -19 percent postcensus pop-drop in this town of fertile land that people got paid not to seed. Median income was hardly half the nation's, meaning folks here didn't see dentists when stings shot through their mouths: They purchased 80-proof Novocain from package stores.

Asa had lived downtown. Near, but not too near, Mother. He liked being one flight up from the juke joint he played, and a safe distance from that woman's grasp.

As I walked, a moan rose up near my old high school, still named after the Jim Crow cracker who toiled for years in courtrooms to keep us out of decent classrooms. He had died; he had won. His school housed petrified books, filled with fossilized falsities or long-dismissed claims. One hundred and eight elements. Pluto as a planet. I couldn't make sense of the glyphs of graffiti on our handball court: PHELSHEPLEHASEPLA. The only art consisted of smeary stick figures, striking dirt with swords or canes. Asterisks covering the eyes.

As I closed in on the moan, patches of clouds briefly covered the sun's glint, the way a bandage soothes wounded skin. When I rapped on the door of the house holding the moan, it peeled back like a can lid. A heavyset man stood in its frame, wearing a wide grin. Only a few teeth remained in his mouth. The rest hung, like hunting trophies, on a length of wire looped round his neck. He chuckled; they jittered. When he gazed past me into that blade of a sun without wincing, I knew he was stone blind.

I offer his greeting here as a complete sentence, though truth is it took me hours to decode: "You, ah, out here offering your hand or your hello? I'm obliged either way."

Before me was Rutabaga Rollins, one of Baldesta's baddest and most versatile bluesmen. Player in any area gig of merit for four decades. Usually he slunk onstage whenever he got the urge. No one chased him off. No one could. He was budge proof, wide like a tuber. With eyes now, apparently, as useless. It occurred to me he'd pawned his vision on cakes and candies. The sugars he was soft on had softened his belly and gumline, uprooting teeth, defeating him in a way no Greco-Roman warrior ever could.

Unsure what my host had asked, I didn't know how to reply. Not that it mattered. Rutabaga struck my ear trying to wave me in. Grinning, he sank his bulky butt on a sofa. Stuffing from its threadbare armrests had settled onto the mushrooming cushions. His hand swept through a tin tub, scooping a beer from a watery basin filled, I suppose, at one time with ice. Amazing the ice in that baking room hadn't sublimated to mist. When he popped the can, its contents smelled of melted crayons. Tepid thing tasted as if I'd opened my mouth inside an active carwash, during hot wax cycle. I was so used to a Rutabaga with working retinas, it never hit me to just dump the beer.

I let him do the talking. He and Asa were musical rivals, and so I didn't want to step out of my role of invisible stranger yet, in case the men never forged a truce over the years. Strapping on a guitar, Rutabaga garbled an intro to his first song, then began.

She scrambled my eggs
Bout half past ten.
Now they sitting so long,
They done hatched they own hen.
Got six little children

Livin here in the shack.
Trippin over they toys,
When they mom coming back?

Flies swooped at Rutabaga's chin, nuzzling beads of perspiration. In the course of shooing them, he dropped his pick. While flailing for it in his massive lap, the moan surged. It hadn't come from him. And it wasn't one moan, but several. I tensed. Crept to the kitchen, bumping a crumpled baby-doll stroller. When I did, the moan shifted into a whimper.

It was Rutabaga's brood. I didn't see them straight off, spotting the skillet before the spawn. Antediluvian eggs, stiff and saffron, sat inside that skillet. Then I saw the kids—none older than five—all twisting up some object. For a dim instant I thought it was the wrung neck of a live rabbit. But as they edged into the light, I saw it was only a stuffed toy they'd torn apart, hoping nuts or candy might spill from the cavity.

Won't you tell me now, mister
Do they all look like me?
Way my woman run round
I'd be happy for three.

After crunching my can and leaving Rutabaga's hutch, I found a coffee shop one town over with semis in the lot. I had figuring to do. Needed to know if anyone was left in town to check on Rutabaga and his brood. If calling in what I'd seen to authorities would cause more benefit or injury. Wanted to sort what I'd seen between sips of brawny brew, and bites of peach pie.

Air from a fan's blades tickled my sweat-soaked ribs. The coolness first brought comfort, then nostalgia: for the town women I'd once had here. Like that one who'd claw my kneecaps as we built to gratification. Or the one over whose bed hung a mirror, warning us when her man's car lights gleamed up the drive. I could finish and shimmy up her chimney within a minute of seeing that beam.

"You fixed, baby?"

I checked my mug—half full, still steaming. "I'm fixed. You my new waitress?"

"Yas, just starting my shift."

I promised I'd be on my way soon, promised not to loiter, but she said, "Naw, your ticket's paid. Fill up slow as you like."

"I thank you, Miss…why, Miss *Embry*, isn't it?"

"Perry?" She switched one pair of glasses for another. "Boy, you done grow. Up *and* out. Must be twenty-five years." Her hissing laugh reminded me of an iron primed to steam cotton. "You know I still get chuckles ever so often, thinking how Asa'd bring you by, in a porkpie hat, singing his music. You were such a fine little sawed-off version of him."

I filed crumbs off my fingertips. "That time's far gone."

"Only far as the tide, baby. Ain't you come here for him now?"

My shoulders rolled, but she didn't catch the shrug. "I'm here for all of you."

"Yas, Asa said you a DC man. I *was* Miss Embry, by the way. Then Mrs. Laird, next Mrs. Pine. Now I'm Embry again. Slipping off names like so many sundresses."

I told her I'd just heard about Asa a few days before.

"Shame," she said, "he can't lay eyes on me no more. Least the Lord's watching him." She wanted something, my consent or comment, and squirted a fresh whipped cream rosette on my pie while waiting. But I sipped the coffee slow instead, to avoid getting into hereafter hypotheses about the man who sired me.

"Shame I missed his service," I muttered, fluffing my whipped rosette.

"Service? He ain't have no service." Embry's lungs wheezed then. She poured her pot's dregs into a mug of her own, so the coffee might carve her rasp. I asked if she'd gone to a clinic. "It don't usually sound bad, 'cept at night. Anyway. Been curious to see how you turned. I coulda turned to him to learn. Yas, you'd be brothers, if you weren't father and son."

"Crossed Rutabaga's path just now," I said, switching topics. "First I've seen him since he went blind. Guess diabetes bested him."

Now Embry's laugh was a cottonmouth working up venom. "His sight didn't get strick from chasing *that* kind of sugar. Rutabaga started slinking around—doing to others the acts he was sure his woman was doing to him. When his lady got sick of it, she lashed him with lye."

"Lye?"

"They *saul* blinded now, baby. Pretty near each Baldesta man, who knows how many, got his sight stole. Women did it a while ago, in a kind of spree, then peeled out of town. The church bring by food for them men. They can't much help themselves. Fact is it's my turn to make drop-offs. Sacks are in our dry-good closet. Would you want to minister in my place tonight…?" She eyed me carefully, killing her coffee with a slurping flourish. "Since you say you've come back here for all of us?"

The wind had whipped up; warm, acrobatic. Cradling groceries, I studied Embry's map of Baldesta's blind bluesmen. First on her list was a man I'd never met. When I poked in his shack, he was locked in a twelve-bar tune, cigarette bouncing on his lip like a diver at a board.

He'd vary verses for hacking, stuff coming out of his throat the tint of poultice. Each time his ash splashed the carpet, I'd kneel to put out the embers. Once he stopped midsong to say, in his combustive voice: "Think you saving Blind Dwight, don't you? Well you dint save shit. Ever since my sight flamed out, my other senses been ablaze. I hear that wind. I can open my door and let it rush in, if some spark get ideas." He patted his coat. "And if *you* get ideas, I keep cutlery on my person. Now, you really like to help, drop a dollar in my guitar case."

I dropped down five. Or tried. Dwight, even in his condition, managed to catch the currency before it landed in his guitar case, flicking his tongue against Lincoln's folded face. Bragging he could tell any bill by taste. "Mmm, a ten. They got tang. That rate rates accompaniment." He dragged out a wooden pallet and foot-operated double cymbal, punctuating his performance with pallet kicks every second beat. Cymbal pedal stomps every fourth.

Dwight sang a three-song cycle, yardstick of his torment: His woman Lizette needed his love; her skin blistered when she lacked for it too long. She in turn made him feel like a man so well, the country home they bought new in November was all busted up by June. They had to move to this shack, since structural harm caused by fierce love wasn't covered in their homeowner's policy. The moment Dwight arrived at his new downtown digs, neighbor men sealed windows so wives couldn't pick up his scent.

Lizette didn't scar Dwight with lye for his lapses. She hauled him to church, to get set right by a right-hearted preacher. Man tried to cure Dwight of his straying, and "It almost worked, that preacher's toil, he nearly torn my roots out the Devil's soil."

But then during a session, preacher's wife paid a visit. *Shoulda seen these hips on hers, man. Wanting nothing but to get clutched. Broad as salvation. A temptation too much.* For emphasis, Dwight dug his uncut nails into my hip. *What could I do but heed the call?* When he did, Lizette took up a copper paperweight of Noah's Ark and clubbed his skull. Then the preacher wrested it from Lizette and took a shot of his own. Dwight saw the arc of one last rainbow in his head, then had seen nothing since.

An anguished buzz filled Dwight's hall. "You keep a pet in back?" I asked. He said nothing. I repeated.

"That's mine and Lizette's legacy."

Unplugging his lead, Dwight steered me to the back. I heard feverish lowing. Stepping inside, I saw a bed by the window, quaking, humming. Its posts chattering against a wall, *luk-aluk, luk-aluk, luk.* A canary sheet atop the mattress twisted into a braid, then shook free again. Now. Will you roll your eyes when I tell you this all happened of its own accord? That there was no body atop the bed to incite it? Or that Dwight's windows were closed, shut off from any groping gusts?

"Jest look," implored Dwight. "Still carries our impressions on her. Shakes its sheets the same way Lizette and me used to make her. Thinking of all them times we worked out our love on her springs. It wants us to lie back on it. How you tell a bed you won't be using it?

"Can't sleep on her no more," he added, removing his hat. "Bed's too sad. Quiets more each month Lizette don't return. A year more of disuse, she'll go completely still. And if I don't soon find some steady vein of money, I won't be long to follow. Hell, you know how it is, Asa. I heard you tried to split Baldesta last week."

"There's been, uh, a mistake here," I told him. "I'm not—"

"I told them church folk Asa wouldn't leave us long. Baldesta is your cradle and cross, man. You could get buried in another town, you'd still find a way to tunnel back. I'm honored you chose my house as a rest stop on your return journey."

Stepping over his guitar case on my way out, I threw in another five.

Again on the streets: The gusts had gone frigid and mean, and were dashing open my excuse of a jacket. Asa was alive. The bitter air paired with my thoughts over this "good news." I dwelt on how he never cut the record that could've launched him out of here. How he never made my mother an honest woman. I thought of Asa's body, drunk, snoring, maybe in one of these shacks, draped on some sucker's borrowed sheets. Hours before, when he'd been dead, he had a lost legacy. Now that he was alive again, so were his failures. I didn't want to face that again. Didn't think if I even found him that I could stand to look. At that wasted life, wasted gift; wasted manhood. Still wasting yet.

Hard winds thrummed the shack windows like angry interlocutors. Each house I came to was occupied with hapless males singing refrains, plinking Jew's harps, hands cupping hidden harmonicas. Because the men were performing before but not for me, with no interest in what I thought, or if I left, I found myself listening to their playing sumptuously, the way I'd eat a dish in solitude, differently from how I would in front of guests, letting all the tones strike me without distraction, the savory and sour and the sweet alike. Each time gusts snapped screen doors shut, the bluesmen would rise, head to their window, and play louder. Sightless but watchful. Sure the wind was their women coming back.

As a boy, I looked through windows for a woman too. Only I hoped not to see whom I squinted for. If I did see her, it meant Mother was wearing her wares at work, spending hours in some stranger's home, larded in lipstick or jewelry that shone like candied apples, that she let men bid to bite off, long as they paid a light bill, or for her boy's braces. In clothes worn to be torn, stitches made for slashing.

Men she never should've put herself on consignment for. River rabble, except, at times, Asa. Who at least tried to treat me as a son, not just what came of his coming.

And on evenings as a teen, I would look through windows of Hash & Burn, the local diner on 61 where I worked. For the arrival of Sharna. Sharna was cheery, chunky. And, better blurt it now, white and blond. Will you believe, though, I didn't seduce her to incite the town? It was her voice, a sweet ether, that doped and decked me.

I'd pull full shifts at the diner after school. She'd work dinner rush with me. After closing time, we convened in secret. Making love in soybean rows, or near catfish ponds, spreading our acts around like crop rotation so as not to get caught. We did that sort of slow-burn sex you don't think much of while making it, but later can't shake, believe you're still living its exploits long after the fact: *Perry,* I'd have to tell myself during my next shift, *stop grinning. Come to. You aren't stroking her sternum, you're shaking salt on an old man's grits.*

Sharna and I were Hash & Burn's open secret. Patrons saw how we shuffled figure eights around tables. Caught me tapping her tummy, which expanded when she sang as if with gestating child. Whenever she dueted with the jukebox, my indifference to her singing had to seem too stiff to be true.

"Cut! Shit, it cut me again."

I looked up. I was no longer with Sharna at our diner, thumb dragging discreetly over her silk blouse. I was instead tracing lines on a woman's glove I'd picked off the next blind bluesman's dirty floor, making one last stop on Miss Embry's circuit.

Beside me, the latest player had just slashed his hand on a tin of cashews. Dawn winked clumsy light on the fresh wound… and several more closed cuts just like it. Scores of pink and beige lacerations scored his chicory palms. Scars like snakes slipping through a farmer's soil, to claim a foolish pullet waddling outside her henhouse.

The smoking queen reserved in my name was in a motel one county over, smack between the airport and Baldesta. My plan had been to do my tour, throw flowers on Asa's grave—if I could find it, and find a florist—squirrel a half pint of gin in my motel room, sleep off said gin, and then flee back to DC.

Instead I'd learned there was no grave for Asa. He was alive. Maybe even here for the finding. Instead, I'd put my dress shoes through tours of duty they weren't built for, straggling all night, shack to shack, in a blind parade of blues that never moved. What braced the men through the filth and helpless stretches, the brushes with botulism? Kept them howling and half starved in their ragged clothes?

I entered my motel. Courtesy continental breakfasts lounged in wicker baskets, waiting to be snatched. My suitcase's rumbling wheels trailed me inside, a hanging bag was bowed double over my forearm, but the desk clerk was too engrossed in solitaire to notice.

"Checking out, sir? Room number?"

"Checking in."

He frowned, scanning the lobby for escorts or harlots. Hesitating to run my card.

"Lost track of time reuniting with friends in town," I offered, as alibi. "Start gulping old stories, I forget to come up for air. You won't be seventeen someday, son. See how it is."

His maddeningly warm grin was proof he considered me no threat, and irrelevant besides. I turned to a kiosk by the stairwell, stocked with tourist pamphlets and placards. Flipping through rows of fliers, I asked the young clerk how it could be that not one sheet so much as cited a bit of Baldesta.

"Why would they? Bit's more than there is to see."

"Yeah, it may seem that way now. But the string of blues songs crafted there were once this region's main cash crop."

"Man…what you want for? Rhubarb pie? Then go here." Shaking his head, he spread out a brochure. "Want to see folks quilt, this place has it covered. Water sports, outlet malls, lunch counters, fishing lures, got it all, within an hour's drive. What they got in common? None are Baldesta. You could go to your room, dunk your head in your bathroom sink, hold it down until checkout, and you'd still be doing a damn sight better than Baldesta."

In my room I stripped quickly. Asked the shower to unbind ropes in my back, an unfair task for plain water. Stroked medicinal ointment over my feet. Applied lotion, bunion creams, gels, bay rum, green tea, and eucalyptus. Kneaded myself. Aired out.

Then I returned to the lobby to turn in my key. "This has got to be a record," said the clerk, helping himself to a mint dish he'd replenished in my absence. "But for future reference? We got a truck stop folks can clean up just as nice in. Would've cost you six quarters instead of sixty dollars."

•

Before my flight back, there was one more visit I needed to pay. Motel clerk was on to something: I'd been holding my breath ever since learning I'd misapprehended my pre-dawn phone call from a few days ago, and learning Asa was still in this world. I needed to go by, pay my respects to a living man. Setup of his shack was the same as the others—tossed clothes, spilt beer. Only here, a Bunsen burner stood upright on a remote shelf.

Ah-uhm (beat), feeling out my feelings
Oh yeah, uh, ah-uhm (beat), feeling out my feelings
Ahm rock bottom with you, we ain't nothing but through,
Ah-uhv (beat), hit the wall with ceilings.

Asa noticed my presence…the sight of his blind eyes winking bent my mind. "Morning. Didn't see you standing there." He chuckled. "Reckon I still don't. You part of the church mission, yes. Bringing along canned goods and unchained gospel?"

"No sir. Well, yes to the can part."

His head, quivering before, shook arduously once I answered. "Only the church ever showed up before. After what I did to my woman—and I did do it, I ain't here to claim otherwise—no one's come by but them. That's been it, for's company goes."

"You think they're—" I stocked his pantry and pulled out a different pronoun— "we're…this whole town is shunning you?"

"For's I know."

He had no idea others like him were scattered throughout Baldesta, that all his neighbors were stricken the same way. None of the men here knew he wasn't alone in his affliction.

"Well, I'm here for you now. Here to see you through anything you can't. How long's it been for you since you lost your sight?"

"Lost count. But my back porch hasn't. Go grab a look."

Piles of newspapers, three years' worth, lay on Asa's steps, bound in rubber bands, ruined by rain. Vines shot between the tri-folded pages; a kind of vine I had never laid eyes on before. I gently pulled one back, pinching a purple flower for my pocket. Headline on top of the stack of papers read: 'Baldoxta Blincness STREtchws

Into Thirc Year.' Thanks to muscle memory and hunt-and-peck luck, that typed story was legible enough. All the other column inches, though, were filled with random letters, alphabet soup strung on a placemat: gYfbjv eljIok lochnister manlexty. Framed by ink-blotched ads, staggered and light-bled photos: giant thumbs. Blurry birds.

"Don't mind my not minding you," Asa yelled, launching into his next number. "I tried leaving this town on my own a bit ago. Tried to go after her." Go after whom? I hoped he meant Mother—I'd have liked knowing she was out there too—but didn't dare ask. "But I barely could stumble for's the depot. And there hasn't been a train to catch here in years. So I turned back home, picked my playing up again. And I got to *keep* playing for…until her return. Until she sees I see her better since she washed my eyes out with soap. Follow? I heard her rustling last night. Rattling my window. For's I know, she testing my faith, doving between towns until I prove worthy of her again."

Dove, I thought, as a verb. Yeah. To exist, without striving, in a state of grace. Mother had had her moments of this. Sharna had too, when she sang. Sharna, who I'd heard had flourished since Hash & Burn. Atlanta, three kids, mortgage-loan officer.

Less than a dot on a map, but all of Georgia for me.

I punctured his can-opener's tooth into a tin of soup, but my host interrupted me.

"No, no, I don't want that," said Asa. "Church dishes that shit out all the time, frying Vienna sausages, cooking pork and beans. Fixing without asking. You want to make something, you know what I'm hungry for. Same thing me and you always liked to eat together. You remember, boy? Still eat those?"

"They don't stock that food where I've gone to live," I admitted. "But I still got a taste for it. Point me to it and I'll serve us—"

"Right there," answered Asa. "Purple-top turnips cooked in neckbone. Scoop me a mess of that, I'll be good to play to you for two hours."

His finger was aimed at a bare pantry, but I knew where those turnips got kept, and so I nodded, and didn't quibble.

Walking back to my car, I had to lean on a porch within ten steps. Ten more, wipe my brow. Another ten, dab the eyes. The ridiculous heat here ridicules: Once the sun sears you to a spot, it's true toil to wiggle away. While resting, I spotted a scorched victim that hadn't found shade in time: a petrifying lizard. Glossy as slate, it'd mistook a dark stone stoop for refuge, a fatal error I understood. If during my walk I had spotted a dendrite, I'd have hoisted it over my head, hoping to unleash leafy shade. Just as even after three years, these men shot useless glances through windows, playing madly anytime they heard a flutter, hoping to lure back the women who'd impaired them.

Of the hazards facing a black boy who pairs outside his race, one is rarely mentioned: when the boy dares to end the romance. Those who simmered silently over my coupling with Sharna did not hold their havoc when I severed ties. Whites who had thought her tawdry for mixing with me rushed to her defense. Up to that point I'd been as respected as a man with my skin and mother's rep could be: apex of a low temple. To spurn that...

Why *did* I spurn that?

I made it through my youth on low-grade craftiness. My mind ever enthralled by experiments, and a drive to possess knowledge before happening upon it in a book. Or at least not accept what limits those books discharged. But in order to avoid the charge of *uppity*, I also hid in convention's quiet shell. Partnering in the chemistry lab with respected but dull white boys. Winning team-based Young Orbiter Prizes in Science, never solo trophies. Pretending to piggyback on the diligence of others. Whites say they want you bettering yourself. But that means you're supposed to grab for what they've already attained. Show of hands: Who thinks *that* can end well?

It was assumed I'd stay in Baldesta, modest credit to my race, my acumen whittled to serve the smug rank-and-file. I could remain at Hash & Burn, whistling, mopping, counting receipts like a whiz. On my way to first black manager of the white diner. This is always how they rewarded our silent striving: allowing the brightest of us entry into the dimmest of their domains: night watchman, sharecropper, ibid., ibid., ibid. Because they despised me, they wanted me staying put.

Still, I might've not minded fastening down. With Sharna. Only it was expected she'd soar away the instant she got her diploma: *That honeyed soprano of yours gonna float you all the way to Hollywood.* Her life was tacit, breathy promise.

As for me? "Your pal Perry can count your royalties. You can trust that boy to balance a ledger." I was supposed to grin. Hunger for the tilted compliments like greasy potato chips. I didn't grin, but didn't object either. I did know about accounting.

What made me spurn her? A disposable-as-shit dialogue, at the tail end of a shift.

"Hey, Perry," she asked, totaling someone at the register. I was on the line, scuffing beef grease off our grill. "Do chop steak come smothered?"

"Just on request. And it's seventy-five cents extra."

"How do I…?"

"Ring up #11, then punch clear twice. Not there. Under 'Special Merch.'"

She did this, then my instruction flew from her mind. If a customer ordered the dish an hour later, I'd have to repeat the steps. I can't say it any different: Knowing this measly truth clawed at me. I darted out for a cig—had to run off. Light up my lungs—with tar and tobacco, sure, but at least some sort of taste. Sharna and I worked side by side. But she didn't know how to ring chop steak, or remember to set the thermostat four degrees warmer with the place only half full. Didn't have the plumber's number committed like catechism to memory. Didn't know the first thing about locking up.

I knew all these things and more. I had to. We both had escape on our minds, but her escaping was inescapable; foregone conclusion. I had to hope she'd follow through, and then take me with her. I couldn't afford being casual about even the breaths I took. She could exhale any damn time she wanted.

At the airport that afternoon, fluffing a travel pillow's gossamer innards, I considered what I could import. Bury Baldesta's shacks and crops, replace them with a grand dynamo. Drown this town, so it might flood others with power: a vernal frontier. The ache and aim of public works. With my signature, I could discharge the refugees, arrange for them to be given a pile of government larder. But how much cash would it come to? Enough to keep the men going? Cover burial costs? I wanted them *seen*... paying them into exile would be an insult to love and loyalty. I should know: A month after the chop-steak flap, Sharna's stepdad angrily offered me a cashier's check to flee, wash my hands of her for good. Slipped it atop a booth I hadn't bused—grease spots quickly came to light—so that one way or another, I'd have to touch it. Studying it, I thought of the anonymous johns laying bills on end tables after lying with Mother.

Yes, his check was an insult. But an insult I took. Took and fled town: first traveling to the Caribbean, to spearfish. It is so alien and lucid there, that deep down. So you dive, again and again, loose yourself from the surface for as far and long as you can.

Later I fled to DC, making my deposit on a place in Columbia Heights.

Pushing ahead with Phase II of my division's study meant meeting many specific criteria. The main standard at this point was my verdict. That the town no longer functioned. Agreed. But it also contains, in this assessor's professional and neutral view, an endangered natural habitat.

One that must be protected under the corps' auspices.

I put in a call to a man on the Heritage and Preservation subpanel. He owed me his career, for splashing bureaucratic Wite-Out over an egregious decision he'd made long ago. I explained how, during my Baldesta tour, I'd come upon a species of *Faboideae* on a porch. Its purple-flowered vine prevents soil erosion, and is remarkably hearty—makes kudzu seem like tender lettuce. But unlike kudzu, it enjoys isolation; its vines grow slowly and tend not to spread. A crucial plant, I assured my man.

I sensed grave nodding on his end. What makes us nod when we can't be seen?

This vegetation, I pressed, demands study, years worth, before we can even consider cleaving the residents from their town. *Yes. Oh yes.* Still making a show of gravity for those strolling by his office, but relieved to have me finally call in my favor.

Like that, Baldesta was designated a Conservation Landmark; given immunity from Phase II's tendrils. Judged well enough to be left alone.

All we needed was a nearby town to swap it with. I told my conspirator I knew just the one. Other than an all-night truck stop and dinky motel, I explained, the town due north of Baldesta has little to recommend it.

Within days of the Hash & Burn incident, I'd turned cruel on Sharna. Humiliating her with flagrant indiscretions, done not for joy, but to frighten her view of our future. Think of the monster I'd have built if we'd wed. Prowling our town regular as police patrols. Sharna would've spent days chasing me out of foreign beds, engaging in wars of speculation each time I was absent, or the wind kicked up strange perfume embedded in my collar. I would have punished her with no fist, no knife but doubt. And who can say how long she'd have allowed my eye to stray without striking back?

No man's fate is a replica of another's. But these musicians' yearning strums, their lashed fingers scrabbling for beans on tin-can bottoms? I know them. To toil in pursuit of your promise, in a town that refuses to recognize you until you get out of or out of joint with it? Of course that puts you in a reckless state when you enter your own home. With a hundred ways to crack and only a few chords to patch you up.

More than I can play, or could have counted on to comfort me in a juke joint. Sharna, I couldn't heal here. To wash demons, I needed to take deep dives, not rely on cold-water-shack showerheads. Needed, to rinse away insults that scorched like sun, more than lye.

STAGE DIVE

THE GLASS ELEVATOR GLIDED from floor twenty to two, exactly one passenger inside. One who knew she wouldn't get what she wanted. Every staff member had instructions to cut Soren Cuevas off. Only newly minted trainees didn't know to warily eye her pre-dawn pilgrimages (as if any dawn, deep in this building's sealed and glowing belly, could be detected). And Miss Embry's searing rasp set those softhearted rookies straight fast when it came to Soren.

"Sno-cones and slush ice are out, after what she did to our cardio room. Produce station's fine. Carving station's fine (try to put her off fatty meats). Pastry Palace and Ice Cream Avenue are off-limits." These words came straight from management's standard script, which Embry toted on training tours, punctuating edicts with whisks of slotted spoons through casserole dishes, to fluff contents and mask built-up crust.

Some plucky trainee would ask about Breakfast Boulevard. In response, Embry would explain that Soren was welcome to any egg, any style, muffins, fruit, even that ugly-ass lox fish that looked like a stacked pile of tongues. Didn't matter, since all Soren wanted was sugar cereal. Which was also off-limits.

This never set well with Embry's trainees, who chuckled with exasperation. *You joking? No cereal, even every so often? That's a cold-ass thing to do to a kid.*

"One, Soren's no kid. She's skidding her way to being grown. Two, nothing with her is *every so often*. Three..." Embry would pause, banging her slotted spoon on a steam tray to clear it and command attention. "...Mister Cuevas say. The only one with a right to *do* some saying."

Soren often lagged behind Embry on her tours, as if she were part of the training. Embry acknowledged her, even pecked her cheek, then went right back to recounting what the girl could and could not raid at the Stage Dive Casino & Resort buffet. "It's not just us," Embry always added, by way of consolation. "Casino crew, the roadies, the pool attendants. We all got marching orders. Folks at Spa-some got fired for giving her too many mud masks, and that crazy internal thing where they irrigate your lower parts like you're a rice paddy off the interstate."

"But Miss Embry, people go here to *get* treated like princesses. Why can't she? What kinda man say he don't want his own daughter to be a princess?"

"Mister Cuevas say."

"You're hard to track."

Soren had located him at last, cloaked by palm tree shadows at Coffee Court, the one buffet section with booths. All other seating areas were exposed because, said the brochures, *new friends are part of the total Stage Dive package.* Truth was security had an easier time preventing food theft with no blind spots and dark crannies to contend with.

"Depends who's looking." He flapped a stick of nicotine gum. "Look sweetie, like I said at sound check: You want to sign me for a private party, text my manager."

She appraised him for the first time since sound check, beyond the concert hall's flattering light grid. He'd held up well. Most of the fallen headliners booked here had unraveled badly in their time out of the public eye—drugs and torpor unetching rugged jaws, smoothing out former Miss Americas' sultriness. His face had retained its shape, though. Until he blew a bubble: Soren was surprised nicotine gum made bubbles.

"Thought you could use some pre-show company." He'd skirted mandatory minimums, serving under sixteen months. Whereas Calvin's mom had rotted in prison since he was seven, with no release date in sight. Soren stroked her makeshift necklace—a coaxial cable missing its plastic shield, awarded her by a bassist who'd been, the year prior, simultaneously inducted into the Rock & Roll Hall of Fame for six gold records and interred in a penitentiary for two counts of statutory rape. "Could you? Use it?"

"What I could use," he began, smile framing the dimple she'd grown up adoring. He wore sunglasses and a ball cap to skirt notice, though wearing them in a dim casino undercut his strategy. Still, the Dimple would always give Drew Dorman away. "What I could use," he repeated, trailing off. Soren climbed in the booth, arranging her kimono (standard-issue in all rooms), cinching its sash to better hike her breasts. "…is coffee. Light, no sugar."

"So get it yourself."

He regarded her cagily—until she added she wasn't allowed near caffeine past six. Then he ambled off, and she felt herself falling out of his focus.

She was blowing this, blowing nine months preparing for his casino engagement; blowing the ten years she'd wanted to touch him. Dorman had been a Disney Channel fixture, teenage star of *Tremble Island*, a mix of mystery and sugary music. The show's premise: after a cruise-liner shipwreck, survivors washed up on a remote archipelago. The vessel's house band turned out to be sleuths. Good thing, since the only other island inhabitants were thieves escaped during a separate, high seas prison transport. The more harried things got for Dimple's crew, the likelier they were to break into riff-heavy pop song, which invariably assisted in putting that week's villain on contrition's path, thus restoring safety and stability on the island.

The image of Dorman fixed in Soren's mind came from a wall poster—winking, Dimple on display, gigantic autograph's river of ink streaming over his boyish chest. The image the world knew was one of blond hair flopping, swollen tongue poking out as ATF agents yanked him, ankles-first, through the dog-door flap of his home meth lab.

"Here." Dimple had returned, setting a café frappé on Soren's placemat. "Now I am your supplier, Soren." A ring of whipped cream sloshed at the cup's surface, an empty inner tube bobbing in the ocean. "How'd you get fitted for that name, anyway?"

"One of my parents wanted Sophia; the other demanded Loren. They wound up mutually punishing each other."

"Sounds like a happy union."

"Much happier since Mom split."

"Messy divorce?"

"Clean getaway. Among us one day, vanished the next." Her mother left without a note, without one clue why, without even taking a travel bottle of conditioner. Like any other guest, any other early checkout. In response, Soren's father had packed the remains of his wife's ditched belongings into boxes, currently stowed in a storage facility two miles off the highway.

"Sorry. And sorry to pry."

"Drew Dorman," she began, after blowing on her cup, "grew up in western Colorado. A Scorpio/Sagittarius cusp, your first commercial was for dental floss, first movie was *Chainsaw Artist*— fourth character killed. When they wrote you out of *Tremble Island*, plotline said you disappeared at the island's outer banks; truth was you were clearing an STD." She tore off a piece of his brioche. "You're not the only one who pries."

Dimple's dimple flashed back. "I've come here to burn that old bio."

"And gamble away a night or three?"

"I'm no card sharp. In fact, I plan to keep after-show festivities dull and private. Who would I call down at the front desk about scoring a projector?"

"For films? Calvin, the concierge. Calvin's your man."

"Gracias, Loren Sophia, for a/v assistance. Can I grant you a request in return?"

"For tonight's show? The song I hinted at earlier. 'What I Could Use.'"

"Shit. You sure slather salt in a wound."

"Better cover up, honey: This whole place is a salt mound."

A salt mound Soren's father had built up fiercely in the last decade, so that Stage Dive could lay claim as a Deep South destination spot, one hosting "the most-recognized entertainers of our time." But the entertainers who booked gigs at Stage Dive were often so recognizable because they'd just finished serving time, either in prison or public pillory. They came seeking both glamour and refuge, came seeking to rehab their images after committing a rogue's gallery of tainted acts: bubblegum bands caught boinking nannies and tutors, a comedian who'd vilified each ethnicity under the sun, unaware his mike was hot, a supermodel who welled up foreswearing fur, only to have stuffed exotic animals turn up in her deep freezer.

"Calvin, good to see your smile."

"Yessir, Mr. Cuevas," Calvin replied, beaming from his concierge desk the next day, as Soren passed through Stage Dive's revolving front door beside her father. "Got to sparkle as bright as the morning. Sore, girl, you are *working* that blouse! How was last night's show with Dimp—uh, Mr. Dorman?"

"Little on, little off. First-night jitters. Oh but Calvin, we met earlier...and he played a song *I* requested. The one that..."

"Calvin." Cuevas pulled out a booking contract. "You need to know we signed that financial hypnotist for October's open date. The Moroccan government accused him formally, but our state department assures me he won't be extradited. The scandal's fresh, which means media circus. But he's living proof of Stage Dive's philosophy..."

"'*They deserve a second chance. You deserve a chance to see that chance happen*,'" Calvin finished. "Sore: You know if our physics test Monday covers the chapter on force?"

"Just stuff on rotation. Centrifugal versus centripetal. But don't ask me to explain which is which."

Calvin peeled off one of the maps he gave lodgers, drawing arrows on it, as if directing Soren to the downtown district. "When something's spinning or turning, one force pushes the object *toward* the center, and the other one, away from it. Know that tight, sick loop the roller coaster at Blessey Fairgrounds makes at the end of the ride? Centrifugal force makes you feel like you're flying off the track, but centripetal force keeps that from actually happening."

"I got the Delta's best concierge on my payroll," said Cuevas, "and he still has time to make honor roll. But did you find time to ask a girl to Dorman's final show? I told you to take that night off, paid, no questions. Free tickets for you both."

"Thank you, sir. I'll keep looking for the right date."

"Discriminating tastes? Good on you, son. I mean to tell you, love the wrong girl at your age, and you'll pay for it when you reach mine." Soren wondered what her dad—builder of a resort that fed off scandal—would think of the scandal under his nose. If he knew industrious, eager-to-please Calvin had messed around with Soren. Only once, sure, and it didn't get far before Calvin stopped cold, re-did her dress buttons. Still. It could happen again. If Soren had her way, it would. Not that she'd ever throw Calvin's career under the bus. And since she couldn't speak of the episode to her father, or anyone who might ever speak to him *or* Calvin, it wasn't really a scandal. Just a part of their lives they kept unlit to others.

"Slut, slut, slut," said Calvin, once the elder Cuevas walked away. "Slut, you bought that blouse months ago and haven't worn it until today. Been saving it for Dimple? Plan to slide into it, and then onto him, ask if *he's* got any requests?"

"You're an idiot."

"But not wrong." He looked in Soren's eyes. "Did Dimple sing

Disney songs dirty for you over coffee? Get you wet?"

"Don't growl just because I had a chance to meet him."

"Please. I met him too." Calvin turned to tidy his station. "Nothing to lose sleep over. He's aged since the show. Looks more thirty-five than twenty-five."

After his mom's sentencing, Calvin was placed in his Aunt Embry's custody. The two kids channel-surfed all summer at Stage Dive, bonding over TV on unmade beds, as housekeeping replenished toiletries around them. Calvin took joy in *Tremble Island*'s production numbers and tinny dialogue. Soren's devotion opened and ended with Dimple.

A sloe-eyed guy approached the concierge desk. Soren had crossed his path last night, part of a six-pack frat crew crammed in a suite. One of a common breed: college kids armed with their first credit cards, set to pillage, dive into desecrations of their own design. His gaze last night had lingered over Soren when he asked if she'd pledged yet. Easy mistake, thinking Soren was in college. She dressed and spoke beyond her years. Even the "Freshman 15" she'd gained was precocious. The frat boy aped ringing a nonexistent bell, while asking Calvin, "Say bud. You got bars in town? Ones those old blues dudes still play in?"

"Yes sir. Who are you hoping to see? Rutabaga Rollins is our most popular…"

"Anyone." He slapped down a twenty. "Anyone with wacky tobacky they can unload for a little profit. Think you can get word to your people we'd be interested?"

Calvin tore a map off the stack like a toilet paper square, circled a block, then covered the bribe with the map and walked away. Soren groaned. If that prick had kept up his "your people" racist shit, she'd have revealed her dad was the man who conjured Stage Dive from the bones of a bereft Delta town. A town that just one decade ago had dispensed more typhoid than tequila shots. Had been home to an open sewer and no running water, flimsy food stamp sheets the only barrier between mass starvation.

Calvin hung up a phone. "Slut, you've been summoned."

Soren's insides clenched. "Dimple?"

"No, Will. Will wants you." Calvin consulted his calendar. "Is this the magical day you and your boyfriend give doggy style a go?"

Soren rolled her eyes. Each month, Will's parents went to a swap meet, leaving him alone. She knew the drill: come at noon, drill Will, then launder the sheets and eat reheated chili on his bare mattress. Was this really how a relationship worked? She should've known they were doomed from their first night, when he'd pulled that stapled pamphlet from his nightstand: *List of All Sexual Positions (Updated!)*. Now, during each visit, he insisted they cross a new way to screw off the list. May was missionary. July had led off with lotus. They'd finished summer with something called The Seagull; he'd pulled his groin.

Will was an insult to the title "first lover." Lips shouldn't feel so heavy when kissing; no one should feel compelled to fold clothes they just peeled off. Bad enough he made making love feel like a factory inspection. But like the tourists who came to Stage Dive on charter buses, Will insisted they try various ecstasies in the list's rigid order. She already knew their precise carnal plans for October, November. Not to mention today.

What kind of love told you exactly how and where it would take you?

With Calvin, it'd be different. If she could only get him to let down his guard again. "That's not hot," he'd claimed, after they snuck into a vacated room with AdultVue still switched on. "She doesn't want to be there. You can read it on her face." Soren was touched by Cal's reaction. What kind of boy looked at women's faces during porn? What kind seemed bored, even insulted, by the sight? And Cal knew from sexy. During their one escapade—in a remote stairwell, vending units blocking them from view—he'd slid cubes from an ice machine down Soren's neck, beneath her chin, along her collarbone. He'd barely even kissed her. Even so, that moment was more sensual than anything in the manual Will had…

"What you thinking about, Sore?"

"Reheated chili." She strayed to the vacant front desk. Rows of plastic room keys lay face-up, designed to resemble playing cards. She shuffled the deck until she spotted a joker, then encoded that card to the digital signature in Dorman's suite. "Will you tell Will I can't make it today? That I'm occupied?"

"Occupied, how?"

She pocketed the joker, strolling off. "Guest services."

"Makes me feel for your father," Dimple said at dinner, spearing pearl onions.

Soren forgot what she'd asked. Something about Dimple's plunge from celebrity, which was embarrassingly hillbilly, but compared to others she'd heard, tiny, quaint. He stabbed a forkful of green beans, stringy as veins. "Having to care for you *and* keep this empire afloat, after his heart got scooped out from his chest." Dimple wouldn't mention her mother directly; no one ever did. She'd fled, claimed a new center for her life, telling no one where or what it was. She'd become a ghost, and no one referred to ghosts by name.

Headliners here fell into two camps. On one side were the embarrassed, gazing at the ballroom's modest seating chart, unable to fathom the divide between their former world, where every blink drew media ink, and this one, where they couldn't even get mention of their names spilled onto "Where Are They Now?" lists. Then there were the cheerful plotters who saw Stage Dive as humble pie they'd force down to get back to the grand feast. Dimple, though, simply seemed grateful. As though life had given him lemons— no sugar or water, just lemons. So he'd sucked pulp, happy to have something besides remorse in his gut again.

"Can I have another pull? Off your drink?"

Dimple's thumb slid around his tumbler's lid until the sipping hole revealed itself. "Can you not call it a pull? Liquor you pull.

Coffee you sip."

This was both, though: dark roast married to bourbon slug. Soren drank, trying to appear dazzled, as if Dimple weren't the forty-fourth fallen-from-grace celebrity who'd slipped her hooch. "Thanks again for asking me to dinner."

"You're good company." He mulled his after-dinner mint. "Full disclosure, though: You're a substitute. Your seat was supposed to be filled by a local I know."

"Are you telling me this local canceled? On you?" She abraded *ossobuco* with a dull knife. How was that possible? Why would any woman not want to hear him, smell him, predict his dimple's next appearance? "Hey. This may be unfounded, but I heard a rumor you got another offer besides ours…"

"A couple, in fact. Harrah's called. Sitcom wanted me for a three-episode guest arc. But those places acted like all's already been forgiven. I gotta scrape back into grace. Stage Dive's a gig gauntlet. Enduring three shows here proves remorse. In a way doing soup kitchen work or drying out in pampered bungalows can't."

Soren could recite the copy sent to woo potential acts: *They showed you the door. Let us give you a window back in. Stage Dive: the second opportunity of a lifetime.*

"And I *am* sorry," he continued. "The things I wanted weren't right to want, but that didn't stop me."

Stage Dive often was the last place that would pay and play the fallen famous, a resort of last resort, ring number nine in the entertainment inferno. A building sealed like a submarine so no actual sunlight—the Delta's great asset—could stab through, with guest rooms offering luxury pillows to soften the pillory. The most fevered audiences flung unshaken devotion at the acts. But more often, crowds gathered to scorn stars, threaten them, see them at their most wretched. They'd treated Dimple that way during last night's performance. Maybe his local friend canceled out of embarrassment. Still, he had to know he was in for a hard response here.

"So what tipped your decision in our favor? Why'd you pick us?"

"This." Dimple pulled a photo from his chambray shirt. Him at eight, with a mushroom cap of blond hair, sporting a ukulele and voracious grin of discovery. "This is the kid I want to deliver myself back to. Got no idea who on your staff dug it up. Shot was taken before *Tremble Island*. Before the floss commercials. Before I became an act. Before I learned entertaining wouldn't be very much damn fun."

She said Calvin had dug up that photo and Dimple nodded, as if this should've been obvious. "The concierge? He's a sweet one. Reminds me of me before *Tremble* began." Soren considered this, gulping her bourbon-coffee cocktail.

She and Calvin were now both the age Dimple had been when he got his TV break. Concerts were Dimple's center; how he'd made a name, a fortune. But he detested them. Until he could cultivate a new center, though, he'd have to keep cycling through his early hits, playing the same moldy, meticulous arrangements. He told Soren that at lunch, also describing conditions at his minimum-security prison; also explaining the vacant look on his face while being dragged through his dog-door. To hear the media recount it, that day was his Rubicon: pop prince charting the #1 song, "What I Could Use," in the a.m., fallen child sensation by the p.m. The truth was, little crossed over in that instant. He started falling long before. It just happened off-screen. All the cameras and sirens did in that moment was shine light and noise *on* the fall, and force his emergency landing.

"These rules are too vague," Soren said in Dimple's suite an hour later, clutching homework and flicking a switch by the bathroom phone. A window above the toilet cranked open, perpendicular to the shaft wall, hard to see, not a true skylight. Most guests figured the switch triggered an exhaust fan. But no, this one let in light and air. Or let out fumes. "On what counts and what doesn't." She examined Dimple's shower rod. A bundle of leather belts looped over it: braided, studded and smooth alike. "Ten belts for three nights? Do you, like, match each with specific pants?"

"I collect, okay? Can you put that one down? Some are… here, we're ready." He gave Soren a pipe. They'd been drinking and smoking weed, a show about English gardens playing in the background. Stones and perennials, perennials and stones. Dimple admitted that dime bags and liquor made him seem not firmly planted on the wagon. But he stressed that for a meth addict, putting pot or bourbon in the system was no worse than an alcoholic letting diluted bitters or Baptist boilermakers pass his lips.

"You think Dad cares what you do? What I do?"

"Well, he's got staff fretting over every ounce of soda or bowl of cereal you…"

"The trivial. Yeah, he's got the trivial covered." She kicked off restlessly flopping sandals. As a kid she'd believed every person she loved cherished every *thing* she loved. Believed, for instance, her dad loved watching full episodes of *Tremble Island* beside her. Soon she learned he was only enduring the show. It was a lesson that stung her then, but now—now that she saw him caring even less about so much more—the knowledge worked in her favor. "Except this place is built and fueled by big mistakes."

"Maybe. But I didn't come to it to make any more."

He stepped around her, for the fridge. Soren sighed. The center of her plan had shifted: She was less eager to hook up with Dimple than to get word to Calvin about that hooking, make Cal envious, make him want her all the more. Tasting her pencil eraser, she resumed her composition essay, 500 words on an indispensable modern invention. But here was her question: When she reported the year her invention first hit the market, its statistics and measurements—did those count as words? Or as numerals, which she was obliged to dock from her sum?

"You're the one, huh?" Dimple smirked. "Who points out the

hole in any truth?"

"If there's a hole in a truth, it's not truth at all."

"Wouldn't that be wonderful." He eyed her. "By the way, you're wearing your robe wrong. I toured Japan a couple times, and you're supposed to put the left side of it over the right."

"Really?"

"Unless one person is about to bury another."

"So undo my sash," she said, arms above her head. "Show me how it should go."

Soren awoke in a gawky position: Still wearing her kimono, but bent at the waist over a mattress. Knees on carpet, face in palms. Elbows jutted, torso splayed over an undisturbed bedspread. She checked her phone to get bearings on the lost hours, and knock slosh from her head. Six texts from Will, the initial ones forgiving Soren's absence, the later ones pleading for her presence now— every hour, on the hour, typical stiff, dull Will.

Cowgirl on Chair will just have to wait, dude. Another time, another girl.

One text from Calvin. Dimple had requested a film projector, and Cal was setting it up after the second concert. Did Soren want to come with, take a gander at the guy's suite? None from Dimple, whose face Soren passed out on following the concert. *Images* of his face, that is. Photos the casino PR crew took of him earlier, posing with table gamers and zombie retirees connected to oxygen tanks. She and Calvin called that group the "slot-bots": They came after cashing social security checks, feeding coins into the machines with zero strategy.

Not that strategy was required at Stage Dive. Visitors barely had to select a desire before it got met. Being here was like holding a hospital bed clicker: tap button, cue morphine drip. Dimple either didn't get the system or didn't care to use it. Earlier in his suite, he'd rebuffed Soren after her line about the kimono sash. Sent her back to her room, claiming he needed to assemble his set list, though she'd seen it lying on his guitar case.

Tonight's show had outshone the first. Partly due to the second-night audience response, which was typically pissier and more prone to castigate than first-night fawners. Headliners who won over second-night crowds were well on their way to a triumphant engagement, and Dimple had done it, bantering with ease, willing to play the penitent performer role, which made the crowd willing to let him move on from it.

But backstage, Soren got zero face time. PR and management cronies saw to that. So she left to squirrel mini-bar vodka, ice popping and quarreling, phone in hand in case he called.

He hadn't, and the vodka finally took its toll. What now? The buzz would only make Soren's insomnia worse. Sleep for her was a slinging sack of cinderblocks, trying to clobber her during one of its passes, but rarely scoring a direct hit.

Soren ripped the crackling paper sleeve covering a fresh room kimono, knotted it, rinsed brutally with mouthwash, then loped to the gaming floor. Dice wagged in the hand of one gambler; ice wagged at the base of another's cocktail glass. A sign read, *Got a Gambling Problem? Call 888-BIG-LUCK*; a number directing callers not to a prevention hotline, but a casino employee paid to encourage callers to disregard their misfortune and cast one more big roll. A banner above Soren, stretched between castellated beams, insisted *Your Dreams Reign Here*. Punctuated by the photo of a grinning woman whose palms received streams of falling gold coins. The model was a dead ringer for Soren's mom. Probably why she'd been chosen. Little pieces of her mother made their way into Stage Dive. Her dad couldn't remove them all. Or more likely couldn't help but let some in. Mom had held her hands like the banner model when she scattered hairspray, aiming its nozzle upward, then fanning falling particles so just enough of them dusted her hair. Did the model say *buffet* like her mother, too? Like two distinct words tentatively meeting for the first time? Boo. Fay.

Fuck, if it was going to be that kind of night, she might as well cram with Calvin for the physics test. He'd have the graveyard weekend shift, after all.

An icemaker cut a fresh sheet, scoring Soren's thought. She heard the ice sheet drop into place, the wire grid carve it into cubes, the minor avalanche into the storage bin. She and Calvin gave a report on this machine. The water inside was exactly 32°F, a temperature where only clean water freezes. Any impurities passed through the drain.

She took a table at the boo-fay. It wasn't time to think about tests. She had to decide what to gamble the rest of her night on. Will? He had fallen into her lap (literally, at a party), was always hers for the having. Calvin needed her dad's money, and would be a monk with her as long as he remained on payroll. As for Dimple, she'd been the center of his day, only to get dismissed.

"Roast beef, sugar?" Miss Embry stood before her in a hairnet, with a plate. "Freshest of all we got. Best too: Chef went mint-wild on the lamb, and the pork loin… didn't hear this from me…is dry."

"One slice." She hadn't realized she was ravenous until Embry sunk a fork in the brown flesh. How many meals had she served Soren? A staggering number. A round robin of hotel-staff foster care had raised her half her life—a shuffle of maids, lobby clerks, masseuses, even vending stockers and pit bosses. Embry had always done more. The trip she'd taken Cal and Soren on, for instance, soon after Soren's mother fled. They'd driven to an expanse of cotton fields, and Soren found herself transfixed by the alluvial plain—the transcript of countless floods, sculpted by nature's slow and uneven hand. There for a geography project, she and Calvin had to halt their work during a downpour; when they returned, the rainfall had vanished, all droplets either burrowed into soil or sucked into the sun's radiating pull. "Does the water always go away so fast?" Soren asked. Calvin and Embry exchanged a look of pity. Yes, she was locked in a sheltered tower, didn't know the lay of land outside its doors; yes, her mother was a runaway. But they weren't supposed to pity her.

A carafe gurgled its ballad of percolation, as Embry placed a hot mug by Soren.

"Is that coffee?"

"Please, child. Hot milk. Dollop of cocoa for color. You know I forbid anyone giving you coffee this time of night."

Soren shoved a balled napkin into the mug. "Forbid? Which one of us do you think people here really listen to? Daughter of the guy paying them, or an old woman, paid by that same guy to fluff buffet trays?"

"You used to be such a sweet white child," Embry replied, moistening her lips. "Girl who asked me about soil spills."

It was one of Embry's favored memories of Soren, though Soren herself hated the naïveté. Years before, she'd misheard the words "this oil spill" on a TV newscast. *But if it's only soil that spilled*, she'd pointed out brightly, *we can vacuum it all up*.

"I'm not doing anything wrong."

Embry chomped an Oreo. "Remains to be seen. But you're a magpie of disaster. Someone *leaves* what's wrong on the ground, you'd pick it up as your own."

Soren fished in her pockets. She still had the copy of Dimple's key she'd made, but had to take a few more bites of beef before bolting. Smooth things with Embry. Not draw suspicion. When Embry had to field protests about the Fresh Catch Court's dwindling oyster stock, Soren, seeing her shot, vanished for the hallway.

Her kimono quivered as the elevator floated to Dimple's floor. She stuffed her clothes behind a trashcan. Outside his suite, a metal bucket held unopened celebratory champagne. The ice inside now a pool of melt. She eyed the water. If Calvin was right about centripetal force, she could pull out the bottle, tie a string to the bucket handle, whip it above her head, and not a drop of water would spill or touch her.

She heard a mechanical trill inside Dimple's suite walls: the film projector's whir. He really *was* watching shows. She'd watched his shows since she was seven, spiraling into crushes, fantasizing for a chance to fling herself onto the altar of his home's master bed (seagrass sleigh, mahogany-stained). Then he had come here. Allowed her to join him on errands, meals, dime bags. Enter his room, rifle his history. She'd come so close to him, only to be sent away just as she was set to reach the center.

Now she palmed his room's card key. Blew out a quick puff and fed the key into the reader, sidling in swiftly—only a crack of hallway light trailed her. Untying her kimono in the foyer, she practiced offering herself in whispers, suggesting he give himself one more night of what or whomever he wanted before commencing his clean slate.

The bedroom smelled of oils and libraries. Dark but for the projector, and the wall on which its beam landed. Soren kept her focus there at first. A child driving a go-cart into a wall. He didn't clinch the wheel to brace for impact, but threw out his hands, shrieking in joyful terror. As the tiny car recoiled he tumbled down onto the rubber track, green racing stripes along his pants, shedding his crash helmet. This was Dimple at seven or eight, years before *Tremble Island*, smiling widely, as in that old photo.

She took a few steps. Dim items began revealing themselves. Full film canisters; empty beer canisters. Items Soren knew tacitly from other rooms, such as sofas, wicker fan blades, bolted lamps. Then what she saw became both clearer and harder to grasp. Dimple, splayed atop a metal cot frame, blindfolded, naked, prostrate. A lanky shirtless figure—male—standing over him. Tufts of chest hair fronting the figure's dark body. *Kiss me hard*, she heard Dimple say to the familiar figure. *Push my chin into the cot until it hits the coils. Don't worry how hard.* Dimple's directions were carried out, scored by dual sets of moans. *Now get me with the belt. The one on your pants, with metal stars.* The figure undid this belt from his loops in one clean jerk. Reared it back, whipped it down. Dimple writhed with the lash. Held his thumb up for approval.

Projected along the wall, the idyllic film spooled forward:

Dimple with cotton candy. Dimple not quite reaching the minimum height standard of a roller coaster. Dimple climbing aboard anyway. Soren pivoted back into the projector's roar of light. She'd seen such light unload itself before, by the river that coursed near Calvin's home in late afternoon, the surface of it flashing first into a bright metal sheet, then piercing her eyes. She saw that very gleam now in Calvin's eyes. Febrile and glowing.

Soren knelt on carpet fibers, feeling around for her fallen camera phone, snapping a single shot without glancing once through the viewfinder, then fleeing. *She doesn't want to be there*, he'd insisted of the porn performer thrashing beneath bad lighting for $7.99 per view, her whimpers like scrapes. *You can read it on her face.* The glass elevator took Soren down, though she didn't recall commanding it to come for her. She had to decide whether to show this picture to someone, or delete it. It was one day before Dimple was due to check out. A day before she and Calvin would take the test on force. But how could she share a captured image she couldn't imagine opening herself? Questions caved in each attempt at a plan: Had Calvin chosen to be there? Or been ordered, a demand made of him behind closed doors? Didn't she owe it to him either way to say and show what she'd seen? Should she bind her lips, swallow the sight? Or testify, spill all, and end this man before he took the stage here a final time? Wouldn't that end Calvin, though? End this entire enclave, Embry's steady work, father's empire? These questions looped inside her, rode her bones like rails. A circuit she couldn't stop no matter how much she wanted its ride to end. Sleep wouldn't release her from it; neither would tending to homework, slugging vodka, or tuning into the TV's dank purr. This was her scandal, now, too: to spin into, or let spin away.

OBSERVING THE SABBATH, PART II

SUNDAY'S SITTING STILL, POSING for pictures, when Richard Stone wants it to hurry the fuck up. He twitches each time Father Jolson lets his top lip rest on his bottom one. Surely now, the Mass will end. But no—there's always another passage to read/prayer to say/warning to warn. Why does Jolson hesitate so long between sentences? All week long, he had one job: Figure out what to say on Sunday. Now it's Sunday. So spit it out, man! Sunshine streams through stained glass, wiggling off gold cufflinks and ladies' silver purse latches. Metal glints throughout the congregation, teasing Rich's eye, the agonizing beauty of light he can see but not soak up. It's nearly noon. The Nets and 76ers will tip-off in an hour without him. Rich's plan to watch all nationally-televised NBA games from start to finish is one he won't let die without a fight. Scratch that: It's not just a plan, it's a hyperventilating dream; a crusade. Jolson better keep that in mind as he bores through what must be more than half of Corinthians I.

Finally, though, the benediction blazes and the choir retires. Rich and his parents move quickly from their pew. The Stones shake the hands and pat the shoulders of the church's slower members, using the physical contact to spring forward through the crowd, toward that glorious oak door and all the promises beyond: the saddle of sunlit laziness, basketball, solitude, and ambition (both admitted and secret).

As he does each week, Rich's father, Jack, suggests Indian

food for lunch. He refuses to patronize most restaurateurs who stay open on Sunday. But the people who run Sonali are Sikh—it's not their Sabbath. At this point in his life, Rich finds his dad's quirks stupid, but refreshing. Like how Jack lets most potential quarrels slide in the hour immediately following Mass. He doesn't argue, for instance, when his wife Marta, Rich's mother, says she wants to skip lunch. She only wants to clean the den.

"Okay, we'll whip up our meal at home," Jack says. "Let's go."

"No, you go eat with Rich. I want to be alone when I clean."

What's she talking about? Who ever heard of needing privacy to do housework? They get daffier each day, the two of them. Rich wonders how they manage to screw up his plans in such quick strokes. What about the game? The fucking game!

But Jack has already, punctiliously, agreed to Marta's request— he believes that this is, and remains for now, a man's world. So what harm, he often asks Rich, can it do to extend concessions now and then to the women we love? "Just one problem," Jack says. "This'll make for a long trip for Rich and myself—first to the house to drop you off, then to Sonali, and then back home."

"You're right," Marta concedes. She wraps her fingers around her chin and hits upon a solution. "I'll ask Lou Canon to take me home. He lives close to us, doesn't he?" Jack nods. "Kiss me quick then. If I hurry I can still catch him."

Unfortunately, Mom following *her* whims leaves Dad free to do the same. At the Indian restaurant, Dad decides to get the food to go. That part's promising—maybe Rich can plop himself and his Styrofoam containers in front of the tube, just as players start lay-up lines. But no: They're going to eat at the library, by which Dad means the New England School of Law—a depressingly boxy building in Boston's theater district, the architectural equivalent of a Swanson's TV dinner. Dad has a big case opening next week, and needs to bone up on the precedents. Rich's teeth grind. Thanks, church. Jolson's homily about throwing yourself into good works must have lit a fire under Dad's ass. Rich explains what precious study time he's missing by being stranded from home, without textbooks; Dad offers back this side trip as an opportunity for his son to seize a grand library's resources, thereby deepening his academic pursuits. Further protest is useless, so Rich shuts his eyes, letting imagination engulf frustration. He conjures a vivid vision of Dr. J posting up Double D, crazy Daryl Dawkins. Dr. J launches an arcing hook shot, Dawkins brutally swats it away, the ball soars comet-like toward the stadium rafters, growing darker and smaller until it is out of sight.

When Dad pops his car's clutch, Rich's phantom players vanish. When they enter the library, morose volumes of brown books swallow the cheers from Rich's imagined audience. In the lounge, Dad reads *The Boston Globe* between bites of pakora and paneer, as Rich licks the souring pickle relish on his fork, dreaming of the score.

"Hello there, lovely."

Ms. Rosalyn, the head research librarian; a day will never curdle completely. Rich's life has new life. In the form of this woman squeezing his shoulder. The contagious green in her eyes brightens Rich's. Her hair falls into her mouth as she speaks, and Rich can empathize; how could anything not want to touch Ms. Rosalyn's lips? Her skin smells vaguely of milk mixed with maple syrup. Rich sketches the cartography of Ms. Rosalyn's breasts in his head, shifting in his hard chair. As they speak, Rich finds himself less and less able to truthfully answer Ms. Rosalyn's questions, the closer she leans into him. From the leap of faith—*by next fall, I'm sure I'll be starting at guard for the team*—to the outright lie—*I have to decide soon which girl I'm going to pick for the spring dance*—Rich is spinning and puffing every answer and remark.

Any reactions on Dad's part are kept hidden beneath the *Globe* pages. Dad won't, Rich realizes, interrupt Ms. Rosalyn. It's not in his nature. After whizzing through the sports section—the lone section Rich wants to read—in seconds, Dad pitches their pages into the trash, then dumps, before Rich can object, his remaining saag paneer on top of those pages, rendering their box scores and trade rumors slimy, stained, unreadable.

But Ms. Rosalyn's smile only grows, encouraging Rich to be loose with the truth. "How old are you, now?"

Fifteen. "Sixteen, practically."

"A smooth sixteen," Ms. Rosalyn adds, tapping a pencil. "Jack, be sure your boy gives a holler this way when he's ready to date."

Jack sculpts his indigestion and bemusement into a makeshift smile. "Clear your tray and trash," he tells Rich. As Rich rises, Ms. Rosalyn's hip catches his arm, his body tensing with the touch. Jack doesn't notice. He just looks at his watch and says, "Why don't we meet up at two o'clock, Rich. You could go read in the basement until then?"

"Sure. I can catch up on current events. Nice seeing you again, Christine."

Jack almost tips the table over when Rich calls Ms. Rosalyn by her familiar name, although she herself doesn't seem to mind. Still, Rich knows his father is a master of gamesmanship, and plans on popping Rich's ego like a balloon with some sort of insult—here it comes—"You carry copies of *Boys' Life* down there, don't you, Ms. Rosalyn? Great. Because Rich has been moping at us for canceling his subscription."

The basement stacks are dark, fusty, and quiet, except for a radiator's clank—not at all like a woman. The only objects like women down here are the soft carpet fibers, the docile yellow of a knit cozy covering the information desk's "Ring for Service" bell, and the Xerox machine. Its warm glow, its purr when it settles down for an energy conservation nap. Rich is leafing through *Sports Illustrated*, but the only NBA article is on the Pacers, and the Pacers suck. They're lucky the NBA let them into the league.

Dad is probably the only person who sucks at basketball worse than the Pacers, decides Rich. He's fucking short and it's his fault

I'm going to be short too. A short piece of fucking crap. Rich rips out a sheet of loose-leaf to jot down his curses. He'll have to admit to them during his next confession, so he might as well write up the receipt. Rich wishes he could play his Dad one-on-one. He'd put on the spin move. Finger roll like jelly. Shake and bake. Into the hole. Ms. Rosalyn would drop by their house (*why* she would, Rich can't account for. Maybe she'd need to pick up some documents from Jack, and she'd hear the ball pinging on the pavement, and... well, who fucking cares, she'd *be* there is the point). Rich would talk trash between drives to the hoop; Ms. Rosalyn would laugh at Jack's paltry defense; the sun would beat down on her head; she'd have to undo buttons on her dress to keep from fainting. "What's the matter," he'd ask Dad while winking at Ms. Rosalyn. "Can't keep up? Can't you play, boy?"

Does a library carry *Playboy*?

Rich grips his pencil, giggling. He tells himself to stop before his laughter attracts the library guard. But it's not such a stupid question. *Playboy* has interviews. With authors. With presidents! And articles, and stories where the woman isn't sweating and squealing by the end. And they review stereos and speakers.

Libraries may be quieter than churches—but they also hold more secrets. There is filth here to be found.

Quasar steered Rich to that truth. Carlos Quasaro, Rich's best friend. His—though you'd have to extract this word from him like a tooth—confidante. At this age every boy needs a friend to tell him it's okay that every single planetary thing—from beer bottles with condensation beads rolling off the glass, to algebra problems that ask you to solve for *x*—triggers an erection or the desire to get one. Every boy needs a Carlos, whose house you can sleep at and whose penis you can compare with yours under lamplight to make sure they're roughly the same size. Carlos—called Quasar because he digs this show *Star Trek* that was so stupid it got canceled in like two seasons—is a bona fide detective. He can sniff out and deliver exciting dust from the most boring places. When Carlos came with

Rich to this library before, they went to the stacks, pawed through pages of nude women posing for painters, and dug up an obscene page 134 from this guy Garcia Marquez. Perverted genius shit. Then they found sonnets from another guy, Neruda. As Quasar translated, Rich felt like a fish dying on a pier. He was flopping in agony, sure, but God, his muscles were burning bright. Rich waited for Quasar to unwrap each word. Each line his friend read was like an actress in a movie slowly shedding her clothes.

But Quasar isn't with him today. And Rich doesn't know great books of art well enough to tell hot from cold. Rich has to forage.

He heads for periodicals. But not *Boys' Life*: fuck you, Dad. Adult stuff. A typed notice on the shelves thwarts his hunt for *Playboy*: "*Select Publications Are Available at the Circulation Desk, to Patrons 18 and Older, With Valid ID*". So Rich pivots his search to *The New Yorker*—New York is kinky, right?—but only finds cartoons missing their jokes. *The Saturday Evening Post* is duller than a Monday. When he finally hits his bull's eye, the dark alley of magazines seem to burst with light; he thinks of the sun streaming into the cathedral, only now, he can appreciate the divine beauty that escaped him this morning, when he was in a rush to leave. Now his eyes have seen the glory.

The glory of *Vogue* and *Cosmopolitan*, titles which sound somewhat stellar. Of *Redbook* and *McCall's*, where the women wear fake eyeglasses and are shown taking care of small children. Rich recognizes the models from *Self* and *Shape*; he saw some of them in *Vogue* and *Cosmopolitan*. In those magazines, they were just looking glamorous; in *Self* and *Shape* they're supine, stretching their calf muscles, or curling small weights with their wrists. Not much of a difference to the common idiot, but a world of separation to Rich: night and day differences in getting to see the same woman in stretchy pants and leotards, or diamante tops and heels. The slight give in the face of this one as she bends her knees to demonstrate calisthenics. Rich imagines a little ounce of pain breaking the plane of her face; oh God. Is this indigestion he's feeling or desire? Didn't

Father Jolson promise that the Lord's charity to Man could at times be unbearable in its brilliance?

When the basement librarian is paged upstairs, Rich realizes he is utterly alone. And why shouldn't he have this basement, and its bounty, to himself? After all, he is falling behind the curve in sex. ed., *real* sex. ed. He's heard that at Robert Kennedy High, the football coach passes out condoms to starters; fucking Protestants have all the luck. He wasn't even exactly sure what a condom *looked* like. A balloon? A rubber finger?

Enough griping; there's work to do. Goods to sample. Rich slithers to a dank corner, where piles of unattended newspapers rise like the stand of trees they used to be, and begins to rip photos of women from the sockets of the magazines. After mangling a few pages, Rich tenses up: He's leaving a trail. What if Mom finds these under his bed? She would tell Jack, who would remember hearing from Ms. Rosalyn how she'd noticed several signs of tampering in the magazine racks in recent days…and that would be that for Rich. Snared in a trap set by his lust.

But he needs the women in these magazines; he can't just give them up.

What to do charges suddenly into Rich's chest.

Instead of tearing pages, he bookmarks them. Picking only photos where the woman's head is turned, or covered by a boa or scarf, or cast in silhouette. He finds he can gape at these bodies only if he does not have to face the face. After he's garnered a large enough harvest, Rich heads to the photocopier, hands simmering. This is a smarter plan: If Mom finds copies, she won't trace them back to this basement. Rich aligns the first woman face down on the copier's glass face. The photo is too large for one page; her ankles and toes will be cropped. This saddens Rich, but he shakes off the feeling. He slides a nickel into the change slot and hears it drop rattle crash. Tattletale noise clanging around the bottom; his was the first coin of the day. He is the only one sinning this way, and that thought makes him nauseous, but he presses on. He hits the

"Copy" button. Motors rev. There is a grinding sound, and the scent of warm plastic lifts from the photocopier. Steam spills from the machine's innards. Then he flips over the product of achievement, comparing it against the original. She's darker at her collarbone, and her nose is a bit washed out, but Xerox has dutifully captured the rest of her, from ripe neck to curved ribs. She is his now, and he folds her, making a crease just below the model's waist.

Rich runs to a change machine, gladly sacrificing a buck for a fistful of nickels. With each copy, each coin, the echo at the bottom of the change pile rings a little less sharply. The routine is a ticklishly beautiful one: apply picture face down, close cover, insert coin, push button, and, like striking a match, things spark. The light flares, the copier reinvents the form of each woman, the earnest bursts of steam rise; this aspect alone is disturbing, for even as the steam warms Rich's nervous hands, it conjures the memory of his mother ironing his Sunday shirt this morning.

Maybe he's the only one sinning this way, here, now. But for all that the people around him know, he's just a teen camped at a library instead of in front of an NBA broadcast. And he is surely far from the *only* one sinning. In thought or deed or some derelict combination of the two. Quasar's sinning right *now*, Rich can guarantee. Maybe Ms. Rosalyn will sin the second her shift ends, or Lou Canon already did, after slipping out of his church suit. For all *Rich* knows, his mother and Jack are headed down that path next.

Rich checks the wall clock. Jack will come looking for him soon. It is time to stop. Rich knows he should wait until he is safely home to review the pages. But he can't keep from peeking, and, in peeking, making pledges. As he climbs the stairs, he promises little promises to the pictures. Promising to take them to bed, sleep all night with them, and to shelter them in the dark space beneath his desk when he has to leave for school or church. It will all go down cleanly. He will stop at nothing to ensure this is a proper affair.

JINGOES

"Beefsteak tomatoes? Oh holy hell," barked J.C. He slid a few fat slices off his French-bread tablets. Glowered at them. "An otherwise perfect po-boy, completely corrupted." But before he could stomp the trashcan pedal to send his would-be lunch to its grave, Gary snatched the sandwich from him.

J.C. steamed on. "Every time we go to that place. Every time! I tell the order-taker that tomatoes give me the gags. Is there universal code for *sans tomato* I'm failing to signal? Does it cost a customer more *not* to get them?"

"That's it," I said, pistolette clenched in my jaws as I reached for a pen.

What's it, mumbled the others, through food-muffled mouths.

"Our new slogan. 'Liberty: It Costs More *Not* To Get.'"

"Almost," agreed Gary. "But swap *have* for *get.* 'Liberty: It Costs More *Not* to Have.'" He popped J.C.'s already bitten tomato in his mouth, then clamped the chunky red wheel with his incisors, as if making a dental impression. Pulp and juice burst from the broken peel, dribbling down Gary's beard, oh so slow. Giving me a jut of his chin, he said, "Good show, rookie."

Before becoming a rookie with Jingoes, I was an old man everywhere else. Each morning, it took me an hour to look like myself. The myself expected by others. Certainly not the self I have become.

On one of those old mornings, freshly hopped from the shower, I opened my medicine cabinet. Shaving lather canisters and eye-drop bottles tumbled paratrooper-style from the shelf. That's when I said goodbye—eyeing all that had spilled, all I needed to apply—to my old self. To my wake-up routine of pills, drops, creams, and balms swearing longevity, restoration, interminable tumescence. To bathroom shelves choked with antihistamines, supplements, antifungal spray, exfoliant to blast blackheads, lotion to lower a receding hairline. Ways to woo joints into suppleness. My firewall against infirmity. I was an adman: I knew the hyperbole of these products to be self-evident, knew more curative juice existed in their jingles. But I bought them, and bought into them anyway, swallowing all their makers would have me swallow, slathering my face and limbs with medicinal marinades.

That morning of my cabinet eruption, I slapped on a dress shirt and took the fuck off. Bypassed each of the highways I took to work and the citrus-and-nectar bar where I blew $18 daily on small cups of infused sap, just to hear my credit card snap through the reader. I skipped all my pre-work haunts, tendered my resignation via text at a red light, and drove on, drove fast, to the home office of Jingoes (only a colloquial name—our official title is Surgeons of Spirit, LLC) with no appointment. A flock of grim clouds tailed me during the drive; watching them slink across my rear-view, I felt the need to out-run the raindrops. Without that hounding storm, I'd have had second thoughts in the parking lot, and those second thoughts might've proved mightier than my first. But to avoid a cold soaking, I launched out of my car and sprinted right up their stairs, past Greek columns, dashing under the portico dry but having left all my résumé copies and references on the dashboard.

"That's fine," assured the assistant manning the front desk. "All we need to size you up for this job is your face. Glasses off, please."

Glasses instead of contact lenses. No lotions or creams. Suddenly, I felt my face's every untreated crease and sag. But after a quick assessment, the greeter's finger curled at me like a scroll, so

I followed him through the empty lobby's echoing tile to an oak counter. "Sign this release," he instructed, presenting a ballpoint pen tethered to a beaded metal chain. A nearby calendar gave the correct date, but for the year 1990. I felt younger already. The building, I learned later, was a historic savings & loans institution in its prior life, sold to Jingoes for a song after going bankrupt.

Beyond the barricade of teller windows, a doughy man assessed a microwave omelet, plucking diced tomatoes from its innards as if they were shards of glass. "You. Ever handle policy?"

"Steered one campaign," I replied, though his query seemed aimed squarely at the omelet. "Pizzallo for Re-election."

"Third district, Georgia?" Meaning to discard just pieces of tomato, J.C. chucked his whole omelet into the trash. I felt proud to be more enticing than the egg. I eyed him full on: pursed lips pushed up at their ends like wings on a bird of prey. A huge hearing aid protruding from his left lobe, though he couldn't have been a week over fifty. Bulbous chin and nose; chunky head topped with fuzz, like an in-season peach. But he carried himself as if he belonged to the same gene pool producing 1950's cinema leading men. Confident fury. I didn't want to look away. Some men gravitate to men they sense can control other men—however that control is wrung: wallet, bullet, or brain. I'm a guy like that. "Impressive. Your incumbent was a dead man walking."

Six points down and two weeks out, when I was put on retainer, I'd figured the only way to keep Pizzallo in office was to keep voters home. Rather than construct pricey ads promoting my man or assailing the other, I formed a committee: Generally Disgusted in GA. Ran a spot showing each candidate in unbecoming poses, along with a voiceover: *Neither guy gets it, Georgia. So why should either guy get our vote?* My ad percolated like a pop song, until poll-booth apathy seemed the only salient response.

Meanwhile, Pizzallo's official campaign sewed up AARP's support and eked out the win.

"We're opening our idea mercantile for the morning," said

J.C., twisting a vault door lock resembling a metal asterisk, and leading me in. "Come, come." As the door thundered shut, the pelting storm beyond the walls went quiet. J.C. turned up a dimmer; a dozen moving bodies were suddenly visible in the vault's dark cavity, scurrying from corners to converge in the center, lunging in suits as if stretching before jogs, some reaching for free weights.

It was a scene I've come to know well: J.C. bringing our group to order. But only long enough for him to bring us all into a collective, full-bore frenzy. As others filed into pupils' desks, J.C. prowled beside a dry-erase board, a Sharpie attached to his pointer rod. "National devotion does more than affect us," he began. "It *enacts* us." He paused. The others scribbled. "Makes us proud. And why wouldn't we be proud of our nation, a factory churning out freedom 24/7? Why apologize for our pride? That's like apologizing for our lungs claiming the cleanest air." More scribbling: I thought the others were transcribing, as I was, J.C.'s lecture. But minutes later, the Jingoes were spouting back slogans inspired by his speech. From time to time, J.C. whipped his rod around, slashing new lines over a point already written.

He brought his Sharpie down to bear on me. An inkblot spread on my shirt's pin collar. "You. Whelp. What made you scramble here?"

To be called a whelp was oddly refreshing: I had two decades on most of my ad agency colleagues, but here I was the rookie. I wiped my brow with a kerchief, then set it aside, wishing I could mask my unease with cologne, aftershave, a dash of one of my medicine cabinet bottles. Instead I swallowed and told my tale of protracted morning ablutions: the patting and rubbing, the applying and removing. The way I smeared myself over and over like some slice of sandwich bread, not in hope of what my balms and creams could do, but in fear of what might happen if I stopped believing in them.

At the ad agency I was being put out to pasture, I added. Young pups there sold product on the basis of soul nourishment. Sold less the idea that consumers must correct their defects than the idea that, by buying, they could amend the flaws we had brought upon the planet. Reparations through retail. Eco-purchasing. That was a party I couldn't RSVP for. *If that was the engine of change,* I said, *then let the fucking thing run me down and flatten my bones.*

As I confessed, a shaggy arm slunk to where I'd dropped my kerchief and moved in inch by inch, evenly, like the tone arm on a record player, finally filching the fabric.

"Hey," I muttered, turning around. "What the fuck, man?"

"I'm good," the guy responded, holding my kerchief to his nose. This turned out to be Gary. Gary, who at lunch that day popped open a plastic clamshell containing my potato salad remains in order to lick it clean. Gary, who, I now know, is a germophile. To toughen his immune system, he grabs all occasions to handle other people's bugs. His untidy hair makes perfect traps to catch bacterial bric-a-brac. He believes that disease is an invention of the meek. That fear of disease breeds meekness. That to defeat disease, you must invite it into your body.

"Years ago," J.C. continued, "being one of us Jingoes was common as a cold. Then we started taking flak; it became wrong to flex patriotism. Show teeth when talking national joy. Nowadays, some overseas asshole pokes us with a stick? We're supposed to shrug. Some across-the-pond pond scum country kicks us, we're supposed to act neighborly, say 'Whatevs, that's cool. *Que sera sera,* man. *E pluribus unum,* my global trading partner.'" I noted the intricate tile patterns where J.C.'s pointer pecked the floor, how the lobby's terrazzo stretched all the way to the vault. As if the money sacks within could have appreciated the mosaic. What beautiful, bodacious waste!

"Manners! Do casino pit bosses emit etiquette? Do loan sharks? Do gunrunners? If you control the entire planet's security and capital, you don't need manners." He drew a ring around my shirt's Sharpie stain. "That's why you come to us at a profound moment, pal. Our mission may have been dormant as a sleeping dog, but we have just been mandated and funded by—well, I can't say who. A most sympathetic syndicate. I'd love to tell you who, but…while we'll be doing legal things, it'd be illegal to reveal who paid us to do the doing. But let me say, they are *gassing* us up with green. We can ditch the candy-ass approach. Slap honest raw-meat nationalism in folks' laps again. In a way, we'll still be advocating *unum*. But we'll define what *unum* is, and if someone in the *pluribus* doesn't like it, they get *le* boot up *le* ass."

The Jingoes quickly came to amaze me. The foot soldiers J.C. recruited were aging, but ten minutes in his presence and they became incandescent with rage. They may have been meeting in secret, but J.C. extolled them to strut. May have retired, but were inspired again to blaze bitterness and fear. Thanks to J.C., they felt potent again in a world starting to treat them as if they'd exceeded their expiration dates. And like any dated item, J.C. could get them on the cheap; they were grateful just to have been taken off the shelves again, and taken seriously.

And they'd done serious work! Before Jingoes, Sid consulted for a coterie of Catholic groups opposed to stem-cell-reliant disease research. First thing Sid did while on the job was burn his job description. "I can't work for you," he'd told his new employers, "unless I derail how you've worked up to now. You picket these groups out of faith. Fine. But when you hold your faith to the light of their deeds, it looks warty, petty." He got his groups to lay down their signs and stage athletic counter-events. Walkathons, swimathons, skydiveathons, benchpressathons. Each "thon" quietly paid for lobbyists to push non-embryo research and grind opposition grants and double-blind studies to a halt, all while Sid's participants came across as fun-loving outdoors enthusiasts, cheering one another on in bright, matching T-shirts.

"Surface frolic," Sid explained to me, "can mask darker waters below. Know who did this well? The Kennedys. Now, they put the damn screws to our country, don't get me wrong. I lived through them doing it. But their takeover of our values was effervescent. Tuneful. They were our political Beatles. JFK was the cute one; Teddy, the wiseacre; Bobby the shy guy. And Papa Joseph was the haggard, Mafia-appeasing sonuvabitch."

Gary strolled in, carrying our newly arrived UPS packages. This was his favorite chore, since it required he touch an electronic signing pen, handled by many hands, that goes unwashed for weeks. "Maybe they were the Beatles. But we're more like the Stones," he said, making devil horns with his fingers. "Hey how *do* the Stones keep their act up, anyway? Get us to keep buying that Jagger, after all his concerts, cock struts, platinum records, and lines of powder and women, still can't get no capital-S Satisfaction?"

"Mick manages to make himself a conduit of our dissatisfaction. If that illusion were to shatter—if his legions of fans suddenly saw him as a knighted dude with a personal fortune valued at over $300 million . . ."

"Then the legion of fans would turn."

"Bingo. Evaporate. As would his supposedly elusive level of satisfaction."

Yes. Our business isn't constructing beliefs, but shoring up shaken believers, reminding you *why* you subscribed to your values to begin with. We connect dots between you and our founding fathers—those canny specters who art in history books and atop currency. We are docents in a democracy museum—PLEASE don't touch the displays—peddling the notion that though those fathers set sail on a great experiment, it's now our sober American duty to keep their experiment in permanent stasis. Let dust gather atop the documents. Consent to any change, alter even one iota of their ideas, and we will desecrate their entire vision.

Now, you may have noticed the prevailing gender of Jingoes. That all ideas and voices have come from men. You may wonder if there is on our part chauvinism or bias afoot. There is not. All men are not Jingoes, but all Jingoes undoubtedly are men.

We've never hired women—not for creative, financial, or support positions. Don't have a women's john in our office. Which would be what exactly: a jane? And we don't plan to accommodate their kind: Title VII and Executive Order 11246 be damned. Before you berate this position, understand: eight percent of men are color blind. Nearly one of every twelve of us can't get our cones and rods right. I myself am red-blind. Our flag's seven glorious crimson stripes? To these poor eyes, they appear a drab, dingy green. What is less understood is female dystrophy, the tendency of women to see shades of grey in excess. Grey will soon be extinct. There is room in our world only for declaration or negation. The reach and weight of info has crushed our planet, rendering it, again, flat as a coin. And as that coin spins swiftly in the air, we must gamble on which side we think it will land, and live with our choice. People like me and J.C., we've made our choice.

We convened daily in our vault, barking like a pit crew, building a set of jumper cables to kick-start pride in the republic. We test-drove, then trampled language. Built immaculate phrases, then bloodied them for sport. Finally, after many months, our results were unveiled: the Red White Blue & Reborn! campaign. Here are some samples of our philosophic slogans:

(Encompassing) *America. Born Here, Born Bright.*

(Anti-Immigration) *We'll Take You In, But We Won't Be Taken.*

(Financial) *Free Market Economy: Our Experiment Worked. Class Dismissed.*

Simultaneously, we erected enormous billboards around the world in places like Dresden and Paris. Panel one of the Paris model was a modern picture of the city of lights with the text: "This is your nation." Followed by a panel of the Nazi-occupied country circa 1944 plus the text: "This is your nation without *U.S.*" We finished off doubters with this simple *digestif* in panel three: "Any questions?" Boo-yah!

In my time with Jingoes, the Dollar has shot up 3.6% against the Euro, and 2.2% against the Yen. Our ad blitz has encouraged favorable trade pacts, reduced punitive tariffs. Our method involves impossibly nuanced numbers and state department rhetoric but boils down to this: Hey, other country! Want your interests protected? Then buy our shit so we can afford to shield you.

But confidence, not currency, is our ultimate coin of the realm. We have framed national liberties so they seem both more (a) concrete and (b) catchable. Focus on selling what people *feel* are their freedoms. Assembly, speech, civil trial by jury, *"where the value in controversy shall exceed twenty dollars,"* as our friend Bill O. Rights puts it? Pfft. Most of us only want to know such freedoms are stored in our civic attic, beside the *what's-it-called* in the junk drawer. I give you these freedoms in their place: Freedom to fritter six solid hours at an outlet mall and call it a productive use of day; freedom to not retreat from assertions, even those easily hoisted on their own petards; freedom to deem all films that don't climax in overwhelming force and fireballs, chick flicks.

Entering the office today—a late May morning—I smell nutty oils and tropical fruits. The other Jingoes are dressed in beach hats and Birkenstocks. Did I forget to check morning texts, miss something about a dress-code shift? As I forge through clouds of bug repellant, J.C. senses my puzzlement.

"Field trip," he explains.

"I never got the memo." I glance at my cohort, who is filling water bottles, cozying to that bug spray. Someone will have to mind the office while they play. Am I the exiled someone? Did I falter somehow? Did J.C. rebuke me? "Was I...not meant to?"

"Stay strong." J.C. chucks my arm. "I kept this trip screened from you because I didn't want you getting edgy. Not only are you going, I want you taking lead." With this reveal, I am restored. More than restored: dizzy with delight (and whiffs of OFF!). Buzzed in the ultimate to have my mentor place in me such trust, the opportunity to take the wheel on this vehicle they've commanded with such skill.

Field trips are where we collect some of our finest nationalist fodder: among you people, in your element.

We don't attend NASCAR weekends, lawnmower races, even political rallies. People at such events tend to merely recycle slogans we dumped into the zeitgeist weeks ago. Sure, it's an ego stroke to hear you echo us, but little more. Where we Jingoes prefer to tread is physicians' offices, or hotel breakfast bars. In such rooms seep the fears and prayers of America. Complaints during visits to ear, nose, and throat specialists; plans laid bare sipping coffee and chomping chalky biscuits in Hampton Inns. We listen hungrily, our ears your Wailing Wall. Relating to you silently, our feverish fingers tapping electronic devices. Testing language by texting back and forth, our faces veiled behind *USA Today* copies, typing tweets over mini-wheats. Would this line sound too twee, this phrasing too hysterical?

For this field trip, we are infiltrating enemy camp. Our chief opposition, ForeverForward.org, is throwing a Memorial Day weekend party at a city park, rustling up more converts to their cause. Our job is to pounce on any chatter running counter to our mission. Persuade their would-be sheep of our might and right. We will be like wild dogs plucking livestock from a farm, damn the repercussions, damn the reports of ranchers' rifles. And J.C. has entrusted me to head our pack.

We the Jingoes saunter in. Scents of slow-cooked BBQ emanate from pits, green eggs, grills, and smokers. We're tracking talk, though, not wings and brisket. Our heads pivot to the prevailing wind, rotate toward businessmen grouped under live oaks, swapping numbers and risk capital tips. I signal for us to split up, assigning one Jingo per jocular chat. It is difficult not to grin, drool.

Can't wait to puncture canines and incisors through that first strip of charred meat. Can't wait to shred the arguments of the opposition, too, though J.C. attempts to temper my temper. "We want to kill the enemy, but don't want them *gone*. Get it? If they aren't still around spreading deceit to potential believers, how can we fortify our own word? Stay in business?" He is right, so right. It mirrors Gary bracing his immunity by gathering others' germs. Exposure to what we loathe will make us loathe it more effectively. We should be grateful.

Though our opposition is technically hosting this barbecue and flag football, they are here incognito too. They want to collect their own slogan-ready language. So both packs float around the park like rival teams wearing identical jerseys and helmets. Each group is in the same standard dress: chinos, Polos, brown belts. Hair parted crisply, if we have enough left to part.

After a few furtive swallows of food, I pick up a bite: a remark from the north-northwest comparing the U.S. empire's current state to the decline of Rome's. My next step is to swoop over, breezily butt in, jaw pressed on my chest so my wire picks up my saying, "Mean-looking frank there," or "Where can I grab me a brew?" But as I am already equipped with meat and beverage, I must improvise: "Heard you gents mention Italy. I went there this year. You know the Vatican fits right inside Rome? Like a little pocket. Only it's *not* Rome! How can you be within something but not *part* of it? Sorry. Don't mean to co-opt your chatter." (Though, of course, killing momentum is precisely my point.) "Name is Ned." (Be a Ned when sabotaging dialogue; it is the least regal name, the most forgettable.) "What we talking about?"

"Bit of shit-shooting," says one of the men, face diffident as a monk's. "I was remarking how Rome wasn't built in a day. But it didn't *die* in a day either."

"Interesting, interesting. But meaning what, exactly?" I try to be amiable, but my question must sound like a bark because the man draws away from me.

The other guy—my enemy—picks up the ball. "What our pal is getting at," he offers, "if I may…is this: What if American grandeur is falling to seed around our ears, but we're bellowing too loud to notice? Our comeuppance has already done come."

I ignore this with a neutral line about the brisket, but the first man—our mutual mark—sets down his BBQ plate and asks to hear more. He wipes sauce from his lip, with the blank look I gave my mirror the morning my medicine cabinet collapsed. He is ready to pledge his loyalty to one camp or the other, and I want it to be ours.

Like we Jingoes, my opponent sells treatment. Sells the idea that something out there is due to get us: a color we're blind to, germ we can't see. For Jingoes, the malady is meekness; for our enemy, it's nationwide hubris and temerity. Either way, not nipping it in the bud leads to an erosion of freedom. "*Freedom*, friend," my enemy says. "We're talking about freedom. We all want it. But wanting it isn't the same as earning it. What if, in our shopping spree for liberty, we've forgotten the sacrifice part of living here?"

"That sounds like Condem-NATION, pal," I tell my enemy. "But you won't do that to *my* nation. I won't stand for it."

"No one's saying you should. But if we collectively exhibited willingness to work for freedom—that we don't expect it to land in our laps—it might inspire other nations to hunker down and construct their own freedoms, instead of trying to tear ours down." I twitch, and my enemy pounces. "Y'okay, bud? Eat some bad meat? You look pinched."

No. I'm regretting not coating myself with OFF!—mosquitoes are slant-drilling my blood. In the vault, we do sets of curls and flyes while pitching lingo. Concentrate our minds by clenching bladders and prostates. It keeps our endorphins blinking. But now I'm too angry to store much longer the watery beer I shotgunned. I'm holding it in, but ideas aren't flowing out. I'm just a guy without his dumbbell, who wants like hell to piss on this river birch.

"Villains *will* come at us," I insist. "You think we can beat off their challenge with Nerf bats?" I know I'm going too grim. But it doesn't matter. Our mark already fled us to reload his plate. Our potential prey has abandoned both my enemy and me, but that doesn't mean we won't go back to barking. His bark, though, is worse than mine.

So when I see J.C. two pits over, sausage link ends flopping off his plate, I wave him over, tap the wire in my chest. I wanted to protect our interests with his gelid snarl, but I don't have the teeth he does. Still: if I hold the fort until his arrival, we'll beat down this clown together. "You want sacrifice? Here's some sacrifice. Know the word 'patrial'? It's a kind of extended warranty for your homeland. Says if your parent or gramps is a citizen of one nation, then so are you, no matter where the stork technically dropped you. Well, I say that's shit. I say our country oughta demand the opposite."

"What the hell does that mean, the opposite?"

"I mean if you fail to be a solid U.S. citizen, then we get to strip your kids of *their* citizenship, too. Export not just you, but all your future and present progeny, out of our borders."

"Okay, that's some severely savage Old Testament shit."

"Not savage: insurance. Demanding you fly straight from day one if we let you in here. How many people would risk their kids' futures on…?" But I don't have a landing gear for my remark. I consult my paper plate for a prompt; except for stray sauce leaking into the remains of my macaroni salad, it's empty. What the hell is taking J.C. so long to come back me up? Even if he can't see me waving my spork, no way could he ignore my chest's popping wire-mike.

Then I hear a strange voice over *his* wire. "See our condiment spread?" the voice asks proudly. "Not a single tomato slice, chunk, or chip in view. That's all for you."

I dart for the dialogue. Who but us knows J.C.'s distaste of tomatoes? Enemy who, that's who: enemies I spot with pocket binocs, standing by a creek bed, chumming with J.C. Who's got his chino cuffs rolled up past the ankles. Who's switched out of Birkenstocks into Italian chukka boots, sweet shoes so pricey they practically require a down payment. Shoes that he only wears for business. I run to him, breathing hard. "Didn't you hear me rub my mike?"

"Sure I heard you. You were in top form. Nice work on, uh, your Rome banter."

"Top form? I totally botched the patrial line you taught me. Were you listening to my encounter with the enemy?" I peer at the others, all holding the same brochure. Not our brochure. "Or have you been too busy breaking bread with them?" I point my finger at his fruitless burger, then his shoes. "Enemy sighted. Enemy *met.*"

"Oh . . . no, hell no. These aren't Forever Forwards. Just guys I know."

"From the yacht club," one says helpfully. "We've gone on regattas together."

"Right. Was thinking of nominating J.C. here as a prospective member."

They all shoot the kind of frozen grins formed for dentist X-rays: muscles rigid so the teeth structure can be properly scrutinized. But the alibi, forced laughter, nervous nibbling at food. It's all mutiny of the mouth, signals of bigger betrayal. J.C.'s been cheating on me. Not with his body, but his values. I demand to know how he can be so two-faced. How he can fake realpolitik.

"Realpolitik? Two-faced? We don't have faces in this business. You, me, we're air vents. We spout climate-controlled rants or tributes to match our clients' comfort zones. What we spout is fog and farce."

It's not fog and farce; it's not.

"Know how I got this?" J.C. asks, indicating his hearing aid.

"Of course. Damaged in combat. It's how you received your Purple Heart."

"I've got no Purple Heart. But before Jingoes, I operated on hearts. For a living. Took in 400K yearly. One day in the middle of a valve replacement, I got hit with vertigo. Could barely bring myself to visualize my incision, cut, or even stand as long as needed. Before long I couldn't place one stent without tipping. Had to renounce my practice." J.C. works a pinky over his incisor to scrub off a pulled pork shred. "Surgery corrected the problem—hell, you've paddled on rivers with me. I do 360° turns in my kayak now, simple as spit. But the operation left me more than half-deaf."

"So you lied to me."

"I arranged for you to hear a pleasing history. After that ordeal, I was through with hearts. Every heart isn't in danger of bursting. But every mind is a mind that can be flipped. A mind someone will pay critical coin to have me change for them."

The high sun hawks J.C.'s forehead and eyes, so he puts on wraparound shades. The kind with temple arms that massage the head while worn. I bought him the pair: birthday gift, Sky Mall catalogue, $749. "Isn't it perfect our rule of law is called a constitution? It's our country's guts. Who cares *how* I define those guts? As long as the bidder for my services wants to digest what I'm feeding."

With that, I rip off whatever restraint is leashing me, and start chasing after him. "Bidder? We aren't at an auction, J.C. This isn't a wrestling match, J.C." He skids on a soft turf patch, and I stab at him with my spork. "You're supposed to believe what you say." Anticipate his pivot, stab again, score a direct hit on his ear. The good one. The plastic tines bend; a drop of blood has formed on his lobe. After the hit, J.C. zips away, scampering into the creek bed, splashing into its cold, grubby waters.

It's shameful to see his chain-stitched, calfskin chukka boots spoiled. But I won't subject *my* shoes to the same fate. Above him, I pace. "Of all the traitorous…I swear…I'd never in a million years commit…" Only I can't finish my curses. They're minced oaths. Because, of course, J.C.'s dissatisfaction was only a mask he wore into the Jingoes office. Of course he stayed on permanent prowl for bigger offers. The others in our pack are faithful to the tenets we talk up while locked in that vault. J.C. could wear his heart on his sleeve because it was a reproduction of a heart. Sure, it pumps. Contracts.

Traffics blood to the proper veins and ventricles, like some freeway system made flesh.

But what he bleeds is the blood of a thespian. Who can die a wretched death, go out after the curtain falls for a three-course *prix fixe* dinner, and then do it all over again at tomorrow's matinee with the same motivation. Have the seated masses eating from his palm. He's a king of performed sincerity.

And a king who has been—now that I've found him chumming around in this compromising position—exposed. Tomorrow I can clear him out. Compose words to assure Gary, Sid, and the others that while J.C. has let down our pack, I can lift us again. Keep our spirits high, our beliefs sharp as fangs. By this time tomorrow, he will be leading the enemy, the throne in the bank vault empty. Mine to ascend to and fill, if I want.

And I do.

"What do you want?" he asks, throwing up his shivering arms. "To tell me I've sold out? Tell me you're dissatisfied?"

At least I imagine that's what he yells. But honestly, his words are hissing past my head, undetected, as I lap up the sweet hickory sauce stuck in my cuticles. Already figuring how I'll redecorate J.C.'s suite. How his disbursements and perks will soon be mine. How the blood I thought I'd drawn on his ear when I stabbed him with my spork is just flaking crust of the same sauce I'm licking now off my nails.

DO THE OCTOBER DANGLE

CONGRATULATIONS. YOU'VE TRACKED THE town terror to her shift at The Cisco. Planning to sic cops on me? Not that the powers-that-be would likely buy your story. Of my story. Didn't mean to make a crime, but it became the perfect one. Or almost perfect, since you 'parently tied the dots together. Want me to spill details over coffee? Kay then, let's sip like the civilized. Only not the Sanka. Buy me a cup of that one, behind the to-go counter. That's our good pot.

Don't pay my manager any mind: It's safe to shake hands. Them things on my palms won't spread. Prick just likes to dig at me, remind me I've been here for years—see the name Linda stitched into my uniform? Means I'm senior. Though actually, in the strict AARP sense, I ain't. In spite of all outward appearances, I'm only forty-nine.

Which parts of my story you already up to speed on? You obviousnessly know I once ran Hidden Cliff's unofficial haunted house. That abandoned, fire-scarred Queen Anne home, located at the spot where our raw waste smacks our river water. What fun it was, at first. Teens streaming in at dusk each Halloween season, admission fees slipped in the mail slot. First few years I only played timid tricks on them: strobe effects; ankle ticklers; black string hung at eye level, so the kids thought they were emsnared in cobwebs.

I had no plan grander than side cash. But business boomed, my imagination followed, and that side of me spilled, I suppose, over. Filled my center. I was able to finance bigger frights. My specialty got to be wiping out guests' sense of balance. I lined walls with slanted mirrors, led kids down a hall with a rotating cylinder, like chickens tumbling on a rotisserie. My mom pitched in—standing still behind hung picture frames, dressed like a courtly duchess. Once the guests' guard was down, she'd grab them through the gilded frames. Other times, she'd wear an all-black bodysuit covered with fluorescent dots. Guests freaked when she moved across a similarly painted room in that getup, thinking the plaster was sliding, or rising, or dripping, depending on her movements. When you want to disorient someone, black is your best friend.

At tour's end I'd dump their woozy asses in the trophy room. Where all my beautiful animals were nailed to the walls or standing on platforms. Not just heads. Full body mounts. Exotic game: hartebeests, warthogs. The occasional vivisected pregnant tiger shark. Bought the entire set from an ancient taxidermist's estate sale, and tended each by hand: stroking furniture polish to gloss up antlers, replacing fallen clumps of fur, and patching up shoulder capes. Over eighty years old, they are. My prides and joys.

I took pride and joy in my entire operation. Even started looking the part of word-of-mouth witch as Octobers piled up. Corns and warts sprouted on my palms and ankles. This froggy hack shot from my throat when I laughed. I didn't mind. I liked the character I'd grown into. But after hosting twelve seasons in that house, one of the rich kids who infest our town tipped city council that I was illegally squatting. Probably got spooked in front of his girlfriend at my show, and decided to whine instead of grow a pair. Our council caved to his complaint—except for you—and voted to condamn the place. In a snap, I went from being Hidden Cliff's Halloween hag to being homeless.

No, hon, we're still talking. I just had to take care of Russo. He comes here to eat during our slow period. Thinks I'm bad luck, but won't say it, or anything, to my face. Each day he orders by pointing at a picture on the menu, which he then snaps shut, like some sprung mousetrap. Ham on rye. Slice of sweet pickle on the side. He hates sweet pickles, never eats them, but since he won't request their absence, on the plate they go. He'd rather waste 1,001 sweet pickle slices than say word one to me.

Anyway, after that screw job, I was homeless. But still in a fighting mood. I mean the one thing Hidden Cliff had plenty of were abandoned homes. I figured I'd convert another into a private dwelling slash spook house. But rich-fuck families started feeling their oats. With each old home they bulldozed to make a condo I had one less residential option, and one more spoiled family to watch spoil town.

At the same time, the Elder Care evicted Mom for missed payments. She'd been declared non-disabled and so thus non-eligible for Medicaid. I'd been counting on Halloween high season to keep me afloat, and keep Mom in a good, warm room. Instead I had to work double shifts at The Cisco serving blue plates, just to afford warm meals for us. Each time she'd play one of her 50's songs on The Cisco jukebox, or I wiped down a table at my station, I'd want to clog my throat with the bleach-soaked rag…I don't know. Sometimes I feel an apparition's controlling me from the inside. Or wants out, maybe, and my ribcage is all that's holding it in check.

Then one evening the high school Driver's Ed teacher came for a bite and a beer. He didn't sit at one of my stations; still, each time our eyes met, he scowled like I'd fucked up his order.

After my shift I slipped to the head. As I made to loosen my apron, I saw half the guy's reflection in the cracked sink mirror (its split side was covered in duct tape). He pressed one hand against the Kotex dispenser and the other against the door.

"I'd like to pay you for your talents," he panted, faucet dribbling behind him.

Well, I remember thinking, that sounds delightful.

My next thought was what if I ripped the duct tape off the mirror? Would glass shards stick to the pieces, the way bugs do on fly-strips? And would I have enough time to grind the shards into his neck and face before he overpowered me? But then he went on to explain he'd been a fan of my haunted house. Said it should've never been shut down. And that he had a new outlet in mind for me and my tactics.

Two beers deep into discussion we were playing one flipper each on the pinball, and he was giving me a nickel tour of pent-up bile. Guys like him like the loop of their own voice as it cycles from rage to joy and back. "I grew up in Hidden Cliff when it started growing in the wrong direction," he explained. "When our only tourism was midnight runs from construction crews in adjoining counties. They'd come rip off our buildings' lumber, stash 6 x 8 planks in their trucks, saw off our good pipes. We were their salvage yard."

"I lived through that with you," I told him testily.

"Yeah? We ever met?" He looked into his ale like it was a magnifying glass.

I unplugged the pinball so its digits would reset, and we'd wind up with the next high score no matter what. "Now we're on the rebound, supposedly."

"Because of them city outsiders? Fuck." His arm sliced the air, cleaving the conversation. "They've made it worse, planting golf courses on the mountain valley. Putting up damn B&Bs and corn mazes. Turned us into a lousy theme park. Flouting checkbooks, knowing we'll wiggle however they want for their money."

"Like Hidden Cliff's their own personal stripper," I agreed.

He smashed his cigarette on the pool table's felt. Watched the smoke rise. "If I just saw you in the right light—I know I'd know you."

So Harris Berg swore. Truth was, back in our Burly High days, we'd had the same teacher seven times. Were lab partners twice. Sang together during a scene in *Brigadoon*. I even joined him in junior ROTC until I saw we weren't going to get to rig any explosives.

Then there was all that fierce looking he did of me while I

danced. Not to Mom's gimmicky, 50's dance-craze songs at The Cisco, or the ballets I wanted to perform in. No, Harris did his looking in titty bars, where I stripped out of nylons on grimy stages, backlit and silhouetted. Back then I was paying for the ballet training on the side, one lap dance and G-string-tip at a time. Those strip jobs were as close as I'd get, though, to the dancing I'd dreamed. Still: even while pole grinding, I found ways to practice. Stay sharp. Do a *penché* as part of my tease. Grab the pole, keep my torso level, plant one leg like a second pole while lifting the other behind my head, like a pair of scissors pulling apart. Clients griped at that, since my exposed parts faced the stage wings, not their eyes. Later I mastered an *entrechat*, leaping, then beating and braiding legs and heels all together, before landing, with a grin, in fifth position. Harris and his boys didn't care *what* the fuck my feet did, long as my tits jiggled. But these prior intimate acquaintances had slipped Harris's mind entirely.

He spent most of our drinking splurge telling post-Burly High combat tales. He'd gone straight from diploma to flag. "Fought for a piece of fabric days after ending my fight for a piece of paper," was how he put it. He'd been great at jungle warfare, because he always hunted one specific gook. He learned the art of still. "Some nights I'd crouch in a ditch for an hour, rainfalls of organs and blood splashing my face. I couldn't outwit my enemy. But I could *outwait* him, and that's why I got out. Why I returned to America strapped under a Starlifter cargo airplane seat belt, not a body bag zipper."

Harris tilted the pinball to end his game on purpose. Told me he was back at Burly High. Buried teaching Driver's Ed. Told me Hidden Cliff's new-money kids were getting in wrecks at an alarming clip. Running reds. Rear-ending locals who'd been making payments on their pickups since those brats were toddlers. "All on my watch," he added. The sterner his lessons got, the more driving accidents piled up on our roads. This cratered the administration's trust of him. Hacking, he lit another cigarette, as if it were just the thing to cure coughing spells.

This is where I came in. He wanted me to turn his Driver's Ed courses into minefields, setting snares and booby-traps designed to spook his most spoiled, reckless kids. I hated those country-club tykes as much as Harris. Maybe more, since with one whine, one of them had evicted me and Mom from the roof over our crowns. Creating a town-wide haunted house? And getting paid while I did it, giving me a chance to drag Mom out of destitute days?

I could not resist.

Harris and I scouted Hidden Cliff locations far from the school's manicured circuit (which Harris insisted to the principal would sharpen pupils' visual cutie) until we hit upon compromised stretches of road. Shadowy embankments, dim intersections, deep ravines, lots of trees or gutted appliances providing cover. We'd plot courses over divot-filled ground, then sprinkle handfuls of rivets around like birdseed. He called me a wizard, said he trusted the homemade matériel I whipped up out of hairspray, acetylene and cream cheese more than he did countermeasures on Chinook copters.

He started thinking of me as one of his enlisted men. Over our four-semester union I ran fourteen sorties. With each success, he moved me up a rank. After each accident we staged, he'd calmly swear to authority types to plain not have seen the nightmarish road visions I constructed. While his students gave their statements at the precinct, Harris kept quiet. Flushed out the enemy with silence. "Let me see if I got this," a deputy might finally say, tapping a service weapon while cutting into a teen's tale. "Your teacher says nothing out of the ordinary happened during your drive. But you claim a man's *brain* ejected from its skull while he was sitting on a riding mower?" By then, I had cleared both mower and brain—a head of cauliflower marinated in India ink the night before—from the site.

After awhile, even the brats would realize their surreal stories sounded suspect. One actually broke down, admitted she'd driven stoned on OxyContin. These sworn statements boiled down to mismatched warfare: decorated Army man vs. sixteen-year-old decorated with acne scars. You know who wins that contest.

Harris urged me to explain how I set my traps. But the only reason you want to know a magician's tricks is to steal them, or spill their secrets to others. Either way, what was in it for me? So I didn't say how I did what I did. Or managed to leave no trace.

For one trap, I hopped into a car with a mannequin's body wedged in its windshield. Drove straight at the student vehicle, veering at the last second and flinging a bloody cow bladder into the driver's side window. The stunned kid—a blond princess with high cheekbones who wore more money around her neck than I ever earned in a month—fled screaming from the car to vomit into a field of pearl millet. While she heaved, I saw Harris peek where I'd hid. Not one spilled drop of bladder blood was there to see, not one shard of glass. I was as happy for Harris's confusion as I was to see the princess puke.

So he just kept slipping me money earmarked for car maintenance, pizza parties for kids who earned learners' permits, field trip funds to the Safe Driver Hall of Fame. I got other perks, too. The first kid we spooked dented the student car so bad the school replaced it outright, thinking it'd be a one-shot expense. I took the vehicle to the body shop, slopped new paint on its skin, transferred the title, and suddenly, my wheezing Hyundai was a spacey Grand Am with less than 15,000 miles.

Harris also fetched me whatever I wanted from Burly High's facilities. Tools and lumber, mainly. When I'd stop by Driver's Ed to pick up my items, Harris's students would often loiter in the hall. Usually boys, rubbing bony, horny fingers across some cheerleader's tits. They'd rarely even glance at me. One time a group of them was arguing whether the Bible considered lust a sin, plague, or commandment.

"People can be sexy and saintly at the same time," this one kid shouted to his prudish girlfriend. "Even the Virgin Mary gave blowjobs."

The others snarled with laughter. "There's a verse about it," persisted the first kid. "Second book of Joshua. Look it up, asswipe."

Oh I was proud to terrorize these fools. Make it Halloween all year, hallelujah. The rush of startling others—being lifted on the currents of panicked air they gasp out—never gets old. But during that fourth, final semester, I made the mistake of hopping in bed with Harris. When he called with his offer, I was in a ratty outdoor shed near the riverbank, where I kept my favorite mounts. Fluffing fox fur and cleaning cobwebs out of the cougar's ears. In a moment, in other words, of bliss. The kind I've only otherwise felt while dancing, or watching someone fall prey to my traps. I should've kept tending my taxidermy. It's not like sex has ever been enjoyable. I'd rather pick ankle scabs. I don't imagine I feel sensations the way most of the world does. Steady pouring rain, for instance, jolts me awake. Infants, which everyone swears smell so sweet, to me stink like The Cisco's dumpster in August.

I never wanted one of those baby things, never wanted to do what had to be done to make one. Really. The sex thing, I ain't kidding. I've loathed every sexual union I've entered into. When I finally agreed to come over to Harris's, it was an act four semesters in the making and six minutes in the doing. Filled with sluggish huffs and collisions. I always tell my body it will like it better this time and I'm always wrong.

After he finished, I wiped the mess he'd made on my thighs. And then Harris started blubbering. A naked monsoon of tears.

I felt cross and tired watching it. "What the hell you weeping about?"

"My son-of-a-bitch son," he said, biting a sweat stain on the pillowcase.

I didn't like, not one bit, that that whole time he'd been thinking about his boy. So I just glared, a glare his pink puffy eyes mis-saw as sympathy.

What a disgusting display. From a Sergeant First Class, no less. I don't care he was naked, still a disgrace to the uniform. I looked in his nightstand for a Zippo; not to strike a cigarette, but to burn his damn ankle. Before I found one, his yammering got bearably interesting. He told me his boy, Bart, became a soldier after Burly High. Harris urged him to become something safer, better, but couldn't point the boy in the direction where better led. Bart got a furlough to come back a few holidays ago. While here, he got blindsided on the river bridge by a kid blistered on a mix of cocaine and beer.

"Hope that boy's rotting in jail," I sincerely told Harris.

"Case was never tried. *Evidence tampering*, they said. That boy hightailed it out of Hidden Cliff the second he was cleared." Slowly, Harris started to separate plastic from wire on a garbage bag twist-tie. "There's a boy in my class this semester, dead ringer of the one who drove Bart into the river. Cory Orr. Reckless. Arrogant. I hate to think who he'll hurt once he's got wheels of his own."

"Dead ringer—?"

Harris pulled out the Zippo I'd been seeking, and lit us a pair of smokes. "Younger brother."

"Well…there are two empty farmhouses we've been saving, on the opposite sides of Orange Site #4. I could simulate a crossfire volley while he drives down the street. Rig a few windows so they'll shatter, make him think he's being shot at."

"That's good. But not enough for this kid." Harris fished out a tall column of hundreds from his nightstand, stacking them on my bare tummy. "Think this'll inspire you toward a more substantial operation?"

"Where'd you come by these," I asked, watching President Franklin's face rise up and fall again each time I breathed.

"This is only an advance." The twist-tie wire was now fully exposed. Harris curled it around the deepest part of his cuticles. "If I can't get this boy off the road, and permanently, then Bart's memory is worthless."

•

Rage wasn't the only thing binding me to Harris. We each had coiled parental stirrings. Not that I'd given birth. But watching Mom's health falter made me feel protective *and* useless. Maybe those words is all parental means. Any rate, my health faltered even faster. I could feel it in my insides. My house was not in order. I wanted to entrust Mom with a life before my own got condemned. Harris's dangled money would put her in dependable home care. The act Harris wanted done for that money would keep me caged the rest of mine. But was that such a bad trade-off? When I'd end Cisco shifts staring at a ceiling fan, wondering what length of rope I'd need to knot one end around the fan, and the other around me, it didn't seem so.

Harris said he wanted Cory Orr taken off the road permanently. Well, there are degrees of permanence. In the time it's taken you to drink your coffee, I've cooked up three ways to give The Cisco's manager a massive coral nary. Pulling off the mission would be no problem. What I was afraid of was how well I'd devote myself to it.

See, my control was slipping. Round the time Harris told about Bart, a scraggly terrier started plodding to my outdoor shed. Stuck its black nose in while I did evening taxidermy. I tried not to think the word *cute*, then hated that I had anyway. Tenderness is a disease. Even when the pup knew I didn't have morsels on me, it still rolled over, let me scratch its scruff. Like it believed it would find no better place than that shitty shed. Like it was happy to be mine. Then one of Hidden Cliff's rich-bitch housewives ruined my dog. Took it in her house, dressing it in clothes so embarrassing I couldn't bear to look. The terrier was ashamed to be wearing putrid sweaters and paw booties. I could tell. May have been starving before, but now it was desperate for dignity. So one day, I bought a tub of liver pate and spooned the extravagance into a terra cotta dish, leaving dribs near its adopted house. Dog followed the trail of fatty meat right to where I was waiting for it, behind the steering wheel of my red Grand Am.

After running it over, I cleaned, drained and dressed it. Drove six towns over to get it mounted. Freeze the body in a permanent pose worthy of what it had been. When the taxidermist saw the terrier's carcass in my gunnysack, he squinted.

"Yeah, I done this," I acknowledged. "Worst wreck of my life, but before this tragedy happened I loved Bart here like a son."

"Bart? Izza bitch, innit?" asked the taxidermist, flipping the terrier on its back. "Annit says on her collar her name was Candy."

"*Name* was Candy, but she'd only answer to Bart. Stubborn like her momma." I handed him another gunnysack with one of my older mounts inside. "Also, fix this'n here while you're at it."

"Good goddamn, a cougar. I heard hunters round over in Hidden Cliff seen glances of these lately. Scat and tracks, anyway. You bag it yourself?"

"No…"

"Found it on the road, then?"

"I bought it from a guy. It's circa 1923. Listen, can you do the job or should I take it to someone who likes cash more than questions?"

The taxidermist pulled his fingers out of the fur, washing them under soap and scalding water. "I'll stuff the mutt," he said, after clearing his throat. "And glue the cougar's paw back. But I hope for your sake you haven't handled this mount much. You know back then they used arsenic on all these things?"

Shrugging him off, I went to get Mom. Since the Elder Care Home booted her, we'd been bouncing in and out of shelters. On warmer nights, slept in my shed. But now it was October in Hidden Cliff. So she'd stay all day in the library, I'd come get her, and we'd scavenge for unattended parking lots we could squat in at night. Eat beans and franks on Styrofoam plates, zapped in 7-11 microwaves, rinsed out in their bathrooms. And her, with bones as brittle as the plastic utensils she used to scoop out her meals.

Mom was beaming when I arrived. She'd dug up a tune we once danced to: "Do the Dangle." A song from my childhood styled like songs from *hers*. From back when dance-craze fads cycled like the moon. One of The Who people, the one with the word "whistle" in his last name, wrote that Dangle song. It brought up the Twist, Mashed Potato, and it made up new crazes too, stranger, darker ones.

For years Mom scoured record inventories, finally finding, in our dinky library, the trophy for her patience. This made me think of Harris: Once Bart's killer got off scot-free, he had—true to his jungle warfare roots—waited in lie for the next best thing. For a younger brother to reach driving age, another Orr he could use to avenge his son.

Couple hours later, me and Mom were in a BBQ dive parking lot, eating fatty brisket, humming to what she'd heard before. With no legal residence, Mom couldn't check out things from the library. Only lose herself in its listening booth. Only borrow their songs in her head. She'd been reduced to that. Songs put her in good spirits, at any rate, made her feel like the good life she'd expected when she first heard this music had not, entirely, given her the slip.

I knew the feeling. I could barely contain my joy preparing snares. Seeing those kids quail in fear. At twilight, strips of ruby filled the sky like pared apple skin. Once the sun slipped behind the mountains, it was time to shine. Still: causing currents of terror was one thing. I did not want to end a life. Even if Cory Orr was bad as Harris claimed. Even though I imagined the older Orr and Bart Berg being school pals, until the world pushed one boy to serve in unarmored tanks, and treated the other to a life of coasting and cocaine. Still. What the taxidermist told me about prolonged arsenic contact spooked me. I knew he was right, that the warts on my palms, the fatigue whipping in me, were signs for what was to come. I wouldn't outlive Mom. Harris's blood money was my last chance to provide her with means. To put her in a proper home. Nothing lavish, like Harris's, with its exposed cement cellar and sky-blue vinyl siding. Just a bed she could turn over in without hitting the cigarette lighter.

"Lin," she said. "Dance for me? This song here?"

She stuck a CD with the song she'd hummed when I picked

her up. Must have lifted it from the library. How she got it past anti-theft devices, who knows, but with all the cameras trained on visitors, it probably meant an end to borrowing days. Sometimes, Mom would tap song rhythms against my car door. I'd repeat them live, to please her. I'd been getting too tired for that lately, and tried to beg off.

"But I like this one so much," she pleaded. "Do it. Do 'The Dangle.'"

Here's a brand new dance with a brand new angle
It's the very last waltz and it's called The Dangle.
You tie a rope 'round your neck and you stand on a chair
Then you kick it away and you're dancing on air.

The BBQ grill smoke was thick enough to provide cover; I got out of my Grand Am and did the steps she wanted. In front of our headlights, I swayed to the music. Swayed in the smoke, and no one could quite make out my face in the fumes.

Lots of brilliant stars the night of our Orr operation—but the fog machine swiped from drama club hid them all pretty good. Once I'd collared Gustin Boulevard with a band of fog, I placed ropes of carrion along the roadside. Finally, student and teacher arrived. Harris put the car in park, then switched seats with Cory, going from driver's seat to shotgun. I used the sick more trees to veil me. Wasn't hard to do in my manufactured fog; a condition I heard Cory Orr complain he shouldn't have to drive in. I can imagine Harris harassing Cory. Calling him a faggy girl. Swearing to flunk him if he didn't start the ignition. We make demands to costume what we dread. Cory gunned the gas, got it to forty as he passed the chicken coop. My snarling cougar mount was crouched beside that coop, and when the headlights trained on its repaired front paw, Cory veered, only to nearly run into what the cougar looked to be snarling at: a full-body cattle mount I'd placed in the middle of the road. Forty pounds of fiberglass, but it looked, in that haze, like a mass of muscle and bone you could only survive by shunning. Here's where I'm sure Harris must have grabbed the wheel and deliberately plunged toward the shoulder. No way the car loses control that bad otherwise. It weaved for a second like an elk caught in a cougar's jaws. Skidding, chassis dragging across black ribs of semi retread I planted. Then it rocked in an unbalanced gallop, crashing into a crosshatched fence I'd spray-painted black.

You want to ruin someone's balance, I'm telling you, black is your best friend.

Once the training vehicle smacked the fence, it spun out, and only Harris's airbag deployed. Orr hurtled through the windshield. Came to a full twenty feet from where he'd come out. Maybe the rumors of tampering are right. I don't know. Don't know cars. If it was tampering, though, I was not the one behind it.

Now listen, I'm gonna play Devil's abdicate, since Satan is surely how Harris sees me now. He'd say I wanted him disabled along with Orr. Point out I had a key to his house. That I knew the layout cold, had a good clue where his cash was kept, and only slept with him to do recon on where he hid it. That I left my snares' mechanics a mystery on purpose. That the less he knew about the battlefront, the greater the chance he might die on it. Kay, well then, why didn't I disable both airbags?

And why, instead of fleeing the wreckage, did I kneel by Harris, run my fingers through his hoary hair, caked with cornstarch? When I told him my trick worked, his lips flattened—the sort of smile that makes its way into caskets. The car's "fasten seat belts" tone played daintily. Cory, meanwhile, was moaning, stretched on his side, twisted into a picture-perfect arabesque, in grass gone grey with night frost. I gave his vitals a once-over. Grackles cawed above, briefly circling, then again flew off. I scoured the roadside until I found the boy's cell, dialed 911, and took off. Only time I'd ever left traces of my tricks behind.

Burly High, to prove how deeply they both griefed and were grateful, lowered flags to three-quarters-mast. The Super Intended swore to bring justice not flowers to the victims' bedsides.

Only they have no suspect, no credible eyewitnesses. I am free, but only because the other major figures in the drama are worse. Orr is out of critical and in a coma. Occasionally responds to noise: pro football, rock music. His hospital bed is near the clinic where I get treated. Last week, doc tells me that arsenic is evicting all good cells remaining in my body. By this time next year Mom will turn *me* into taxidermy. Least she'll do it in the comfy Elder Care home. Now don't give me the eye. I took from Harris only what was promised for completing the fright. For a mission accomplished. Didn't clean him out, I'm not loaded, just got choices, is all. Either force Mom to witness my health dangling lower and lower over the next year, or do what the Dangle proposes. Agree to close one night at The Cisco. Find a chair, make a noose.

Anyway. Dinner rush is starting. So, if you aren't turning me in—are you? Fine. Then I better memorize the specials. Appreciate it. And the coffee. Those other assholes on Hidden Cliff's council couldn't be swayed to attack the problems of this good town, but you? You always gave visionaries like me a little rope. A little hope. Whichever.

As for Harris, well. Unlike Orr, he's mobile. But not a well man. His scars healed, but the head trauma goes on. You know he lives and butchers by The Cisco? I come there often, waiting for him to place me. Pull the memory of my face from the fog of his mind. He hasn't yet. But he's taken a shine to me. Or maybe pity for my condition. I can't say: It's almost impossible to tell when people you pity, pity you. When I stop by the shop, he slices me a half-pound of venison sausage with his gleaming carving knife. Puts a little extra disc of meat, free of charge, in my hand with a bashful smile, like I was an utter stranger. Can't say whether I hope it stays that way or not. On the one hand, if his whittled memory returns, I'm sure he'll cast me as the villain in our ploy, and shortly after, some squad detective will fish my lopped head from our river. On the same hand, that could be exactly the kind of friend I need right now.

AFTER THE JUMP

ONLY WHEN THE DAUGHTER soothes Seth Snow's skin does he feel the pressure beneath it. Seth spikes at June's touch, eyes shut as she works him over. He hasn't been aware of the twinges, though they've been building in him a while.

Seth's back is, in June's ten-year-old opinion, a jagged mess. "And your neck's a rock pile," she marvels, briefly patting that area, then going back to the back—trapezius first, next the quarry down his spinal column. Patiently gauging where she'll do the most good as Seth grimaces, belly down, atop the garage workbench. It's the garage of a tool jockey, a man who welds and solders, rivets and planes. In this garage where so much has been built—there's June's first field easel, her brother Joyner's old crib—it's easy for Seth to imagine June's pounding hands as an excavator's claw, loosening boulders in his shoulders, bashing chunks of crust into stone, then those into pebbles, those into dust, at first coarse, and later, finer and finer...

Seth winces, and June stops. "Too hard?"

"Don't let up," he responds, drowsily. "It feels like tapping."

"Like what?"

Tapping, Seth repeats, demonstrating on his neck. His words come out softer than they should, reedier, the result of partial vocal-cord paralysis, which make him sound perpetually parched, as if dust went down his windpipe. Strangers once offered him water when he spoke. These days, they dole out lozenges.

"Bad week?"

As June finds a rhythm—sting and lull, sting and lull—Seth considers saying why he's so tense. Revealing how the trouble that her mom has gotten into may trigger a countdown of their last days together. Only it's gratifying to not be on edge, to savor the aches breaking. "A bit badder than usual," he says instead. A hiss rises beyond the driveway. "We better head to the misting. Your brother and mom are waiting. Got your card?" June pats her pocket. Seth gazes through the garage's grimy window. "Gonna be a full moon tonight."

"I know," June says, dashing dead a no-see-um on her knuckles. "But it's never full enough to see Dad."

A map hangs from the belt-sander hook, one including images of all twelve lunar colonies. This month's featured colony on the calendar is the colony June's dad now labors in, an omen Seth wants to ignore, but can't keep from seeing.

Subdivision denizens are already lined up around cul-de-sacs. As if waiting for a shuttle, or to be admitted into a show. What they're actually waiting for, though, is dusk. Dusk and droplets. For jets of water to curtain their bodies with oscillating streams. As Seth and June race by, Tim, from two doors down, chucks Seth with a porcine fist. "Thought you were gonna miss your dousing, man."

"Miss what I live for?"

The two trade tired grins: The line is one Seth would say at Tim's liquor store, if he still bought gin from there just before closing. But since booze's alchemy depends on water, it hardly is an option for anyone anymore. Liquor hasn't quite been prohibited but is certainly prohibitive. Tim's costs nearly eclipse his profits. More customers than ever want stiff belts but, thanks to this mess with the moon, fewer can afford the remaining stock. Liquor, liquor everywhere and not a drop to drink.

But other, drier vices are still floating up for grabs.

"They knock off that guy you're working on yet?"

Seth shakes his head. "It's scheduled just after midnight on Monday. Only the president can pardon him now."

"When you draw him croaking," Tim says, "do me a favor. Under his picture, sign 'Good Riddance.'"

As Seth and June step close to the sprinklers, none of the other residents gripe. But make no mistake: Seth's an interloper. Residents of this subdivision—one of the few that can afford a weekly misting—guard their privilege doggedly. Residents at Seth's meager apartment complex only get to herd in a barren pool once each season. Stand atop its baking concrete crater as the landlord soaks them with a fire hose. Seth has paid rent there ten years. Works check to check as a courtroom artist for federal cases—a final frontier where film crews cannot tread—sketching hot-button trials, how defendants appear on witness stands once damned by the light of their lies; how aggrieved victims react to judgments.

This work makes Seth feel like an elevated caricature artist. Viewers expect to see crags of defiance in guilty faces. Heavy lines early in trials, elation later, on the surfaces of innocent skin. You see his pastel sketches inserted in online articles "after the jump." How we adore comeuppance! It's worth scrolling or clicking past endless pop-up ads in order to see the look on son of a bitch X's face when he learned he'll *pay* for what he did. The neighbors wish that kind of comeuppance for Seth. They view him as a moisture moocher. If he weren't shacking up with the moonnaut's missus, he couldn't afford to live here. And if they knew how friendly he's been with me—his current, guilty subject, the most notorious moisture moocher—they'd wish even more comeuppance upon him.

But Seth's staying is Sylvia's call. Even with him in her house, its population remains at its pre-moonseeds quota of four. May be deplorable, what they're doing, but it's legal.

"Dad-B's back is screwed," June reports, mist dancing on her fine arm hair.

"Language, June," Sylvia responds, but there's no gravity to her gruffness.

"Screwed tight is all I mean. God, I wasn't cursing."

"Ease up on your mom," Seth says, though truth is, he isn't feeling charitable. He hasn't spoken to Sylvia all afternoon, not since having to pick up her and her belongings from work. But now the water emerges in a heavier mist—a maze of vapor they'll all lose themselves inside. With the droplets comes relief, a slight springiness, as if this is some supermarket mister writ large, refreshing all the wilted families like bunches of kale or rutabaga. A little mist won't restore the brown, matted front lawns, but it does restore the homeowners. Beads float over them, catching dusk's last light: Soon everyone glistens under its wet net, like they've donned party clothes. The water's sweet electric scent eases body odor and curtness, the festive atmosphere undercut only by nearby policemen standing guard with truncheons.

Drops cross Sylvia's and Seth's faces. Looking her way, he sees the sting of regret in her eyes, the frustration in her tensed brows. "We'll work it out," he mouths to her. Sylvia reads his lips and, thankful, draws close, offering her moist lips to his.

"You two are gross," Joyner says, a reference to their gentle kiss, not the grime.

"Your dust's not coming off," Sylvia tells Seth. Meaning not general dust from the general day, but powdered pigments from Seth's soft, fat pastels.

He wipes a blade of vermilion off his cheek. "Drawing's due."

"Drawings do *what?*" Joyner asks, clasping spray in his palm like lightning bugs. "They're not alive. How can they do anything?"

Sylvia and Seth giggle over the miscommunication. They laughed this way when they first met, effervescent, easy. Droplets hang before them, held aloft by warm air currents and lack of density. Sylvia playfully waves at the mist, as if dispersing gnats. "Do shoo, dew." Now the whole family has caught the giggles. Can't help it. Water seeps into a desiccated head, and the head gets giddy. Happened in spaceflight, when Sylvia's spouse broke from Earth's gravity, his body water redistributing to the sinuses, producing puffy light-headedness. Happens to Sylvia after gulping Percocet.

Seth knows neither sensation.

The misting continues beyond the usual stop time. Has a water surplus been harvested? No—it's the reverse. Forecast calls for major fluid ebb. People need to hunker down for the coming drought, like bears fattening for winter.

"Are they saying severe?"

"No, exceptional. *Exceptional drought* this time."

Seth steals a gaze at the marauder moon—cold pearl, robber baron of rivers—as it emerges in the sky. He is grateful for the sight. Sure, during the prior planetary *exceptional drought*, a population equal to Louisville, Kentucky, died from dehydration, but still, he is grateful. *Keep drying us up*, he thinks. *Long as it keeps* him *up there*.

To think we thought our moon might make a perfect mirror of Earth.

A carnival mirror, in fact. We launched our initial moon transports years ago, their bellies plugged with supplies. Former oilrig and pipeline laborers followed, along with skilled contractors, like Sylvia's husband, and engineers, like me. We'd developed an enzyme meant to generate moisture: We were going to grow water. Early setbacks didn't tamp our plans, or audacity. Soon as a few safe pockets were secured, wealthy tourists joined us on brief excursions in tiny cabanas, drinking earthrise cocktails, exhuming wallets while our vehicles trod and tromped.

Science, business, legislative, ecological leaders: We all blazed with belief that colonizing the moon could help ease the swelling crowds on our planet. So pleased about altering the moon that what the moon might reflect back didn't enter our thinking.

Workers like Sylvia's spouse carved open the moon. Drilled impacted-basalt basins, plains of volcanic maria, inadvertently carting back home millions of dust flakes from a now-hardened ocean of magma. The dust—inaptly referred to as *moonseeds*—stuck to uniforms, equipment, adhered to fingers and bodies *handling* uniforms and equipment, and made its way to water sources on earth. Turned out moonseeds salinize fresh water, impregnate it with crystalline salt deposits. Imagine invasive plants capable of sparking drought. Imagine beach sand clinging to a shoe, reproducing rapidly, leeching more moisture with each germination, reducing some of our largest bodies to withered appendages. Lake Superior? Half-lost. Louisiana wetlands? Bone-dry.

I voiced early concerns about the dust we dragged back. For saying my piece about Earth, I got reassigned *to* Earth; an alarmist Jeremiah. Now I've been proven right, but am *still* a failure; twice over, in fact. First, because I failed to sway the initial skeptics that they had made any error to begin with, and later, because I stole from them to rectify the error they finally copped to.

Seth Snow told me he kept up with my case, but never deeply. He had a job to show for. A family to raise.

A family that became his, piecemeal. First member was Sylvia. Leaving Tim's liquor store one night, Seth looked up from unlocking his car to see soft moonlight glance along her bell-shaped jaw. He'd seen her in this store before, but the pieces didn't snap quite into place. Because the Sylvia browsing aisles on other nights had done so while gripping a man's hand. On this night, she only gripped a bottle that reminded Seth of an Oscar trophy.

"What kind of drinks," asked Seth, "can you make with Frangelico?"

"Earthy ones." She gazed at Seth's feet. "Are you…wearing sandals with a tux?"

Close. He was supposed to be at a gala with his girlfriend, but had forgotten to pick up his shoes with the other borrowed threads. Now the rental place was closed, and the gala, which they had to skip, nearing dessert course. The mild extravagance of liquor was meant to smooth over a rocky argument. Things were getting a little heavy with this girlfriend, though. If she couldn't see the humor in wearing flip-flops with formalwear, did he want to wear the relationship's weight around his neck much longer?

"Open-toed shoes usually make Tim nervous," she said. "All that glass in his store."

"He probably appreciated that my flip-flops are black. It's the little efforts."

Seth and Sylvia's trajectory moved in an ordained arc. Drive to his place, put on music, put out drinks, tell a few tales from his repertory, and…hours later, escort her from his apartment with a grateful, final kiss. He'd forgotten how small the effort one-night stands—the hummed tune in sex's symphony—required to jump into, then away from.

As he walked her to her car, moon still visible, he was doubly happy. Happy to have gotten laid, sure, but also to have leapt from a laborious union into a light one. Within a month or two, most memories from this night would evaporate from his mind. So he thought. One light night turned, though, into a blurry month of sex at his apartment on Coming Street. In place of plans, he and Sylvia cracked jokes: *Yeah, here's my place on Coming Street…no, not there*, there, *oh yeah*, right *there*, right *there*, right *there. The realtor says on Coming Street, it's all about location, location, location.* He never asked why they always went to his place. Never looked closely at the darkened recesses of her car's interior, which would've revealed crayons and stuffed animals. Made him ask questions, made her reveal that a sitter assigned to all moonnaut spouses was caring for her children. Sylvia never volunteered mother or marital status, and if it wasn't volunteered, it didn't, so far as Seth saw it, exist.

"Fill up fast, guys," she says now, as the group shuffles back from the misting and shuffles out dinnerware. Thanks to Sylvia's slip today, a Child Protective Services agent may visit. She's probably hoping it happens. A visit might mean another chance, an opportunity to throw herself before the court's mercy.

"What you bring us, Dad-B?" June asks, watching Seth hoist a translucent sack. Joyner first coined this frustrating nickname for Seth; with June joining her brother's usage of it, it's a label that's clearly going to stick.

"Chinese freeze, from off the highway." The meal's been sitting in Seth's car for hours, but refrigeration is redundant: Few restaurants bother serving fare that spoils anymore. They arrange themselves at the table—Sylvia sitting where her spouse would have, Seth in Sylvia's spot—divvying various freeze-dried chunks and strips, dyed to look as they would if fresh: egg roll (desert sand), General Tso (russet), bean curd (cream), squid surprise (charcoal). Last time Seth got to-go, June and Joyner fought over portions. This time, he's taken no chances. "I ordered extra dim sum."

Joyner jostles the sack, doubting Dad-B on the dim sum. The six-year-old's bond with Seth has always shown strain. June's been the easier sell—on Seth's presence, pledges, even this switchover from fresh to freeze-dried food. Eating freeze is an option now. But soon it won't be, and June understands the need to get used to something alien early. Adjust to doing without. Our initial goal was to cart all our luxuries to-go to our neighboring satellite. But now, to conserve H2O, we eat astronaut food on Earth instead. Freeze-dried Chinese has proven a delicacy. The sodium-paste strips approximate sauce, liquid. The hardened plum sauce's reflective hue reminds Seth of the lake he once fished bream from. A place where Seth could draw away from his father's demands that he learn a trade, quit wasting summer months drawing faces at pools.

"We have a working pool. In my correctional facility," I told Seth, during our earliest chat. Once my trial ended, we were permitted to speak freely. "Got caught heisting water, and I've been sentenced to one of the last prisons left with a pool. Is that funny or grotesque?"

He sought *me* out first, but I kept asking him back. To learn about his accidental family. The stories poured, once he saw how thirsty I was for them. He'd tell me about routines as minute as dinner cleanup, as teaching a boy to grip a baseball—routines neither he nor I had known before—and they left their tread on us both, an impression that wouldn't lift.

Joyner says little at dinner, jetting to his telescope after fulfilling his required bites and comments. "Can we draw water?" June asks. The two have been sketching Seth's evaporating childhood lake. Tonight he plans to teach her how to capture coruscating sun, the tide of light when it strikes water's surface. Seth will feed June bits of memory, which she translates into images. Her talent exceeds his at that age, though he wonders if June's devotion to drawing will stick around once dating and boys begin to weight her world. And will Seth even be around to stop its departure?

"We need to neaten," Sylvia says, frowning. "I want the house looking its best."

"What for? Who are we trying to fool?"

Seth isn't sure if June is just being brassy or knows something about the trouble brewing. If she is throwing a challenge at her mother, it's not an errant one: Junk skirts every surface in the house. It would take all night to make a dent.

But Sylvia's hope of making amends moves Seth, so he tells June they'll conduct art lessons later. He heads out to install replacement roof shingles in the dark. The clouds are terrifically uncooperative, blanketing the moon's fat face of work light. A rainless tropical storm is to blame for the shingle shakeup. All gust, no downpour. Something like what this affair was supposed to be: all steam, no substance. When did the substance arrive? When did the affair become adultery? When he took Sylvia to bed? Or when he discovered she belonged in another? And has it *remained* adultery? Can Seth claim—now that he's taught Joyner to throw a four-seamer, and monitored iffy areas in June's report cards, all things the man upstairs didn't do—mitigating circumstances?

Or does that only amount to so many appeals meant to get him off the hook?

I know Seth questions such things, but I'm unsure why he

does in my company. Why he willingly spills any detail I ask for. *The moonnaut's clothes: Do they still hang in his closet?* (They do.) *Did Seth ever try on the sweaters and shirts?* (Yes, but never in view of Sylvia.) It's possible Seth has no fear of judgment from me. What's the harm in telling transgressions to a man in a prison jumpsuit, running out of breaths to inhale? Coming here may prove, in where I sit, that my misdeeds always efface his. Or maybe he doesn't hold me in judgment. I've never asked how he'd have voted if he'd sat on the jury. Maybe I'll ask before midnight Monday. Maybe I'll let it die a mystery.

Seth begins slapping in a few replacement shingles, confused by the sudden illumination guiding his work; the moon is still wrapped in clouds. Surveying the area reveals the new light source: the kids' bathroom skylight. He peers through Plexiglas at Joyner and June, weighing themselves on a scale. "I'm down to seventy-two." "I'm up to fifty." They convert their findings into moon weight. "It's too late for you to go, June," Joyner determines. "They don't let moonnauts receive more than sixty earth pounds in one shipment. But I'm getting bigger. I need a rocket to take me there quick."

"They're not bringing you up."

"Why not? They said under sixty. That's why I didn't eat my extra dim sum."

"You aren't cargo, idiot. You're a life form.

"But I need to be with Dad. Not Dad-B, Dad!"

"You're only saying that because you can't remember him. If you knew who you were missing, you wouldn't miss him."

Seth is grateful to June for that remark. But he also admires Joyner's goal. He knows by heart Kennedy's call to "conquer" the moon by decade's end; the hard choice made because it is hard. Watching that speech now is bittersweet. We have a new lunar clock ticking down: simultaneously racing to the moon while trying to dodge the damage it caused down here. If we don't bring moisture back to our blue marble soon, our cradle of life will convert to a cavernous desert. Meanwhile the moon, meant to be a high-end resort planet, is being built up rapidly as a camp for affluent refugees.

Knowing H2O would soon outrival crude oil as liquid currency, I began, after my forced reentry, hoarding it. I wasn't much of a hydro-bandit though, leaving a big, fat trail. Jury barely took an hour to deliver a verdict; the judge immediately sentenced me to a correctional facility until my execution could be arranged.

Why do you call this a correctional facility? Seth once asked me. *And not just prison?* Semantics, bub: I'm amused that's what *they* call it, while offering me no way to correct the behavior.

So you'd reform? If they gave you a chance?

Touché, I told him.

Seth refused to reform too, shacking up with Sylvia after he met her kids, and after he learned her husband was in the brackish heavens. Even after he saw her doing her best, through powders and pills, to ascend in her own right. The husband still remains Sylvia's spouse. No divorce papers are allowed for moonnaut marriages, even if there is a claim. And there is a claim.

That's another reason Seth sought me: I'd crossed paths with Sylvia's spouse. His trail was notorious. Not that dicking around up there was rare. I'm not here to claim sainthood, understand, just because I bolted beyond the clouds. That setting is Alaska frontier, with foxhole thrown in, to the nth degree. Enough laborers were killed or injured in accidents—the detached-helmet incident being, of course, the most horrifying—to plant this calculus in our heads: You can die any day. And *since* you can die any day, do you really want your bed to have been half-empty the night before?

Sylvia's moonnaut slipped orbit four years ago: rotten dad, alcoholic, treated her like dirt. To neighbors, that all gets eclipsed by the fact he's there, suffering interstellar ailments, earning scads of cash to be deposited into June and Joyner's accounts upon completion of mission or life (should moon exposure end him, they'll clean up double).

Moonnauts are heralded profusely for their service: automatic heroes no matter how low a life they led down here. For jury rigging a new home to rescue us from this one, laboring round-the-clock to provide an emergency exodus from shortsightedness, they receive our eternal blind praise.

"How will it happen?" Joyner asks June, in the little capsule of their bathroom.

"I don't know. I guess they'll tell us where we can live."

"Here or the moon, you mean?"

"Joyner, lunar travel isn't an option for us. And I doubt Dad's coming back. But if Mom's not allowed to keep us anymore, he just might legally become our main parent. Make all the big decisions about us from…you know…from out *there*."

The kids, Seth realizes, are conspiring about what he and Sylvia tried to conceal. He wonders if the moonnaut contacted them on the sly, a satellite call when the adults' backs were turned. But he reconsiders: Of course Joyner can sense dinner table tension. Of course June can read wary faces. Of course they want to know if they'll have any say in their next destination.

"If we're sent away from Mom, will Dad-B still get to see us?"

"I don't know. But if Mom can't see us, I bet Dad-B stops seeing Mom."

Stunned, Seth wonders how June could have reached this view. She's jumping to conclusions, believing one break means an end to the family unit they've built. Or Seth's irritation with Sylvia's lapses is more evident than he thinks. If not for love guiding him, he'd have given up on her months ago. Each time Sylvia veers, he's been there to correct her course. Holding her head over the toilet bowl. Deleting texts, shredding notes from suspected dealers. Trimming back a dusty orange grove by the fence so she couldn't do a line there, under darkness of grimy fruit globes.

"Quit." Seth looks into the Plexiglas. Joyner is succumbing to his own vice, thumb-sucking, and June is none too pleased. "I said quit it."

"It feels good and you can't stop me."

"Maybe not. But it's disgusting. Makes your skin all bumpy.

Bends your teeth. And you know better."

Seth couldn't watch Sylvia constantly, couldn't trace her dark side everywhere. So when she got fucked up at work, got caught cowering in the custodial closet, and instantly got her walking papers, he retrieved her from the office, tried to sober her up before the children leapt off the school bus. Hid her from them until she had.

Hiding. Seth knew it well. The lake was the lone place he could escape his dad's wrist slaps, back shoves, repeated judgment. His way of leaving the planet. Seth fell into his job. It wasn't premeditated. He started sketching his dad, in a lark during his lake visits, as a sinister thug, enjoying a bitter laugh with each completed, snarling face.

What I did wasn't premeditated either. The first water I took, I took only for friends and myself. It was only later I began arranging for mass illegal transport—black-market deliveries to nations in no position to endure the drought or purchase "credits" needed to secure water from countries with the means to stockpile it. It's become an arms race with agua that everyone must enter. But the nations least able to keep up could least afford not to. Were the ones that had nothing to do with colonizing the moon in the first place. Got nearly 230,000 gallons into needy hands and mouths before being caught. I know. Insert your *drop-in-the-bucket* remark now.

Seth has drawn me throughout the process: arraignment, trial, verdict (he's very impressive, though I didn't know my forehead looked so domed since its hairline receded). He'll sketch me for a final time at 12:01 a.m. Monday—the first execution for water theft and fraud, an act deemed sedition. But he's practiced in advance of the big event. I've peeked at rough sketches, curious how he imagines I'll look at the end.

It's my first execution too, I remind him.

Seth climbs down from the roof, joining Sylvia to clear the dinner remains. The unfinished freeze-dried ropes and paste strips look bumpy, wrinkled, the way the American flag appeared like little more than a shirt in need of ironing in early moon surface shots.

"Finished up there?"

"Hardly started." He clears his throat, deciding not to scold Sylvia, or repeat what he overheard on the roof. What good would come of either reaction? Instead he says: "I do noses and expressions, not cabinets and wiring. I'm not as handy as…the former man of the house."

"Oh yeah, handy. The former man was plenty handy."

Seth drops a tablet into a jug, then switches on the sink spigot. The jug fills with opaque liquid, then shuts off automatically. Suds fizz as the household's allotted weekly drinking water agitates against this tablet, making the water potable. "If the court denies…," Seth starts to say, shaking the jug swiftly. "If we don't hear good news, maybe you should reconsider reconciliation? Please. Listen. That way you'd still keep the kids, the home. We could still find a way to…more or less maintain what we've got. With his track record, he's not coming back. Not with all the action he's getting up there."

She jams a spatula in the jug and stirs. Turns on the stovetop fan to circulate noise, keep the kids from hearing. "Reconcile? Give him that satisfaction? Ask for mercy from a bastard who tightened my lungs, sucked my oxygen for most of our married life? Who's gone hog wild with no repercussions? Platinum member of the 230,000-mile club. He's known as the Lunar Rover up there, did I tell you?" Before the moonnaut left, Sylvia had been on the verge of leaving him. If she'd done it then, she'd have been excused, even commended, by most. Now she's the villain. "Can we drop it? We've got to get this place in order, in case the court plans to send someone by late…"

"Sylv, you're having a come-to-Jesus moment." He watches fizz break, sediment sink to the jug bottom. "But how much is that moment worth, since you already jumped the cliff?"

"Oh, so sorry. Sorry for trying to keep us all together."

If she wanted to keep them together, why'd she act so stupid? Why leave the coke in her compact, imagine the dust on its mirror wouldn't be spotted by someone, and then *wouldn't* drift to her boss, parole officer, estranged husband? "Maybe it's time to pay the piper. Accept some share of the blame."

"What did you say?" she asks. But she doesn't need a repeat; his voice was clear. A miscommunication maybe, but not missed communication. She storms into the next room, dim sum residue still on her fingers.

A drawing of June's rests in the family room. One of the lake he hasn't seen. She must've drawn it after dinner. God, her vision! The way she thought, at ten, to capture not only the reflection of a figure fishing, but to leave that reflection quivering with light where the lure strikes the water. Technique's coming along, but just to have the idea. Seth feels his own hand quivering—not with excitement but a strange charge of dislodged rage—as he reaches for her sketch pad.

"Pick it up."

Now *he's* the one needing a repeat. Pick up—what? He looks away from the pad to see Sylvia aim a phone at his face. Didn't he hear the ringing? It's someone calling from the court; the judge has reached a decision.

"It's for you, Sylvia. You're the one who has to answer."

Sylvia nods, cups the phone, blows on it a moment. Then she orders Seth to at least get on the hallway phone. Hurry: She can't face this news without him. Seth *does* pick up, but with his back to Sylvia, so she won't see that he's holding a hand over the receiver. He doesn't want to hear the ruling. He'll be able to see Sylvia's face from the hallway mirror. See it widen with relief or constrict in pain, and that is all he can handle.

The defendant's reaction, after the jump:

A ruling is always a blessing to one party and punishment to the other. But it doesn't always fall along the lines and loyalties a witness would expect. Seth Snow has sketched faces he guessed would register horror but instead were colored by relief; pardoned faces continuing to defend themselves. Even those sitting on the same side of a courtroom respond differently. Best friends, family members, failing to reflect one another's reactions to rulings.

So it is with Sylvia's face, when she learns she cannot keep her kids; that she will, come Monday, lose custodial rights to the court, and they will be legally entrusted to a man living eight earth circumferences away. Her look is an imitation of composure: the moment where self-possession grinds to powder. Tranquility's last stab.

That tranquility will disappear for stretches in the days to come, then show again when she visits whatever facility the court exiles June and Joyner to, or when loose acquaintances approach, asking how are those kids, does she have pictures on her? Oh yes, pictures are all she'll have on her. In days to come, Seth will sketch Sylvia's aped composure over and over, until wrist nerves deaden and his hand feels free of weight. He'll draw so hard, fine powder will spill over a towel lying in his lap, permeating his apartment carpet, pigments no solvent could remove. He'll lose his deposit. Dust from each sketch fluttering off his fingers, onto prior drawings he has put aside.

There was tension in Seth's face when the call came, near his brows, and edges of his lips. It may have looked similar to hers, but was not a mirror. His spiked the moment hers vanished from her face. His has been in constant orbit since she hung up the phone. Orbiting questions he's fated to ask in a vacuum. Will he take steps toward Sylvia now, to help her pick up the pieces of what she helped shatter? Or leave her completely? Because, when he looks at that last lake drawing June drafted, one he scooped up just before the state scooped up the kids, he realized June was right. All that effort he's made these last months hasn't been for Sylvia. The affair only amounted to putting one foot in front of the other, a quick tumble into bed, a predictable and small step.

The giant leap, the fall into love? That happened with Sylvia's kids.

In a minute I'll turn in this tale, then prepare for 12:01 Monday. I know you'll be there at the scene, rendering my final facial expressions with your pastels. One small bite from a needle in my veins, and I'll attain escape velocity. Before that, I'll request lobster Newburg and peach bread pudding for my last meal; the facility will send in its stead imitation crab and apple compote. I'll ask for bottled water too. Why not? Did I hoard what was precious? Yes. Will I pay for the crime? I will. Would not taking have been a larger crime? My answer to that is the reason I'm here, and won't be this time tomorrow. So forget tomorrow. The moon, at this moment, slants through my window; its glow floating past the bars, spreading an elongated rectangle of itself onto the concrete, the shadow of a shallow, glowing bed. Do you remember when moonlight was romantic? I'll lie atop my cell's smooth cold floor gazing at that glow all night, until it becomes romantic again.

ACKNOWLEDGMENTS

Stories in this collection previously appeared in the following publications, and were honored and recognized by the following organizations:

"Where You Get Ahead of Yourself" in *Epoch*—cited in *The Best American Short Stories 2012* (Tom Perrotta, guest editor)

"These Are Our Demands" in *The Cincinnati Review*

"Frequent Fliers" in *The Good Men Project*

"Layover" in *New Letters*—winner of the *New Letters* Readers' Choice Award

"Absolutely, I Remember You" in *Michigan Quarterly Review*—finalist for the *Glimmer Train* Very Short Fiction Award

"A Thief at Either Side" in *Southern Humanities Review*—winner of the Dana Award in Short Fiction

"A Damn Sight" in *Conjunctions 62: Exile*

"Observing the Sabbath, Part II" in *New South*

"Jingoes" in *The Chattahoochee Review*

"Do the October Dangle" in *Cimarron Review*

"After the Jump" in *Conjunctions 64: Natural Causes*—special gratitude to illustrator Kevin Somers for use of his drawing

Thanks to the terrific staff at these publications. Grateful appreciation goes also to:

The publisher: Victoria Barrett, Andrew Scott, and Erin McKnight for ferrying pages into a home;

The editor: Bryan Furuness, who championed these stories for what they were, and challenged them to become more;

The colleagues: at TCU, and previously, at Penn State Altoona, Illinois College, and Hendrix College. Special thanks to the Claridge and Hendrix-Murphy Foundations for their generous support;

The friends and readers: especially Kimberly Miller, Alex Lemon, Jamie Poissant, Tyrone Jaeger, Hasanthika Sirisena, and, for their insights into ballet and haunting, respectively, Katie Faulkner and Sarah Pitt Kaplan;

The DNA: my parents, for staying on-call through it all.

ABOUT THE AUTHOR

 Matthew Pitt is the author of the previous story collection *Attention Please Now*, winner of the Autumn House Fiction Prize and finalist for the Writers' League of Texas Book Award. Stories of his have received numerous awards, are cited in *The Pushcart Prize* and *The Best American Short Stories* anthologies, and appear in *Best New American Voices, Cincinnati Review, Oxford American, Conjunctions, Epoch*, and the *Southern Review*, among other publications. A native of St. Louis, he lives with his wife and daughters in Fort Worth, where he teaches at TCU.

Photo credit: Leo Wesson